Tommy
And the P

Table of Contents

Copyright and Disclaimer.. 4

About M. R. Gerbo 5

Author's notes.. 6

Dedication 7

Chapter 1 - Long Night... 8

Chapter 2 - The Home... 12

Chapter 3 - East Porch 17

Chapter 4 - Rosie 26

Chapter 5 - Ms. Haverhill.. 47

Chapter 6 - Lumpy.. 55

Chapter 7 - Cap Visit 61

Chapter 8 - The Posse... 64

Chapter 9 - Tommy 71

Chapter 10 - Breakfast 77

Chapter 11 - Lips.. 82

Chapter 12 - The Rescue... 86

Chapter 13 - Pallbearers 91

Chapter 14 - Lunch 95

Chapter 15 - Miss Sissy 99

Chapter 16 - Mabel 106

Chapter 17 - Julio... 111

Chapter 18 - Abuse... 116

Chapter 19 - Jimmy... 122

Chapter 20 - The Movie... 126

Tommy Two Pockets
And the Posse of the Marsh

Chapter 21 - Rumors 133

Chapter 22 - The Boot.. 139

Chapter 23 - Gettin' Otis... 146

Chapter 24 - Out and About 160

Chapter 25 - The Threat.. 171

Chapter 26 - Crow Island... 177

Chapter 27 - Kidnapped... 181

Chapter 28 - Left Behind... 186

Chapter 29 - Marsh Journey.. 188

Chapter 30 - Trapped... 199

Chapter 31 - The Posse of the Marsh 207

Chapter 32 - Rescue 217

Chapter 33 - Goodbye Party... 225

Chapter 34 - Fricke Island 235

Chapter 35 - The Source 243

Chapter 36 - The Next Week 252

Chapter 37 - Enough 256

Chapter 38 - Lips Service... 264

Chapter 39 - Senior Chief Petty Officer Springstead 269

Chapter 40 - Change... 278

Chapter 41 - Island Days 285

Chapter 42 - Fishing Posse 289

Chapter 43 - Investigation.. 300

Chapter 44 - Julio's Point 305

Chapter 45 - Cap Comes Through.................................... 309

Chapter 46 - The Find... 314

Tommy Two Pockets
And the Posse of the Marsh

Chapter 47 - Family 320

Chapter 48 - Time for Sleep 329

Tommy Two Pockets
And the Posse of the Marsh

Copyright and Disclaimer

The front cover is illustrated by James Sullivan.
Contact at: jsullivan@shutterpointmedia.com Instagram: @ @sullyvangogh

Edited and published by SWL Media and Learning Center.
Contact at: www.swlmedia.com   swlmedia@outlook.com

About M. R. Gerbo

M.R. Gerbo grew up in Michigan near the western basin of Lake Erie and spent much of his youth fishing and exploring the inland marshes. His career as a business executive took him to Iowa for most of his adult life. He now lives in Florida with his pretty wife of 47 years, Dr. Joan.

He has always considered himself a writer and can now capitalize on the joy he finds in the written word. When not on his lanai writing, he can be found on the pickleball courts, in his wood shop, or playing with his band, the North Loop 4tet.

Author's notes

In October 2019, my wife and I were with our friends Tom and Connie Filip in Northern Michigan to see the beautiful Upper Peninsula fall colors. One morning Tom came out of their cabin in Sault Ste. Marie. He was wearing a shirt with two pockets. As we both like to rib each other at every opportunity, I started calling him Tommy Two Pockets. Somebody in our group said it sounded like the name of a book. Could have been me, I don't know.

As we were driving around, I started thinking about it. I was right in the middle of writing Fricke Island, and I had written a quick blurb about two Lake Erie commercial fishermen finding a body in the Lake. I went back and revisited that and decided that it would be a good place to establish the character and his ability to be a world-class smart alec. So I expanded that in a chapter called Tommy Two Pockets and introduced my readers to Tommy Two Pockets and his buddy Julio.

Tommy Two Pockets is two intertwined stories. One from 1920 in the small Hamlet of Black's Bay and the other in 1987 at the Mouillee Rest Home. The events of 1920 were still affecting lives 67 years later.

As I was writing this book, I dealt with friends and family suffering through their last days on earth. That changed some of the direction of the book.

I hope you enjoy reading this book.

Dedication

This book is dedicated to one of the bravest men I have ever known, my friend Tom "Two Pockets" Filip. He is the reason we now live in Florida and the inspiration for this book.

Tommy Two Pockets
And the Posse of the Marsh

Chapter 1 - Long Night

She kept running the words through her head.

The sleeping pills knocked her out for a few hours until the pain overpowered any respite they gave her. The arthritis medication was useless.

Her back was on fire, so she went through the ordeal of turning from her left side to her right side an hour earlier and was still working on it. At least she thought it was an hour. She couldn't tell for sure. The face of the clock was just a pink blur. Last week, she received a shot for the Macular Degeneration, but it wasn't doing much good. Her right eye had some peripheral vision sometimes.

If she could just push that left leg over. She could grab the handrail on her right and turn a little, but now she was stuck. She tried calling out for help several times but knew it would get lost with all the other people on her wing wailing through the night. The attendants didn't care anyway. She believed the rumors about a poker game that went on in the wee hours.

Occasionally, she would hear someone walking down the hall with their loud shoes. She didn't know what they were up to, but they certainly had no intention of looking in on her.

"Why did Lucille have to retire?"

She was the only good night attendant. She'd roam the hallways listening and doing her best to help if she could. She would cry with them and had some good meds. She didn't know what Lucille gave her, but she was happy to get it. They were illegal for sure, but she didn't care. They worked. All she had to do was put a $5 bill on the bedstand next to her lamp, and she was all set. Lucille put it in her mouth and held her hand while she chewed it. She could feel the drug go through her body and relax the muscles and joints and let her fall off to sleep. Blessed sleep.

Lucille told her she could never talk about this to anyone, but she must have had lots of customers that didn't listen, because she would hear the whispers.

"Talk to Lucille.......Let Lucille know.......Lucille is an angel......I wish I could afford Lucille's magic more often."

But she never said a word to anyone. Her son asked what she was spending so much money on, not that he cared. He was just curious.

"Ma, I just gave you $200 last month. You need me to get more out of your account?"

"Mahjong gets a little expensive, my dear."

"Well, as long as you're having fun."

"I am....I really am."

After Lucille retired, she came back to visit once a week for about three months, then she stopped. Marvella said her grandson, Detective Martin, told her Lucille wouldn't be visiting anymore. He wouldn't say why, but it wasn't hard to figure out. There were a lot of long faces at this news.

Tomorrow was her birthday. 85 years young, as some of the well-intentioned idiots would say.

Tommy Two Pockets
And the Posse of the Marsh

"Trust me; it's 85 years old, my dear."

She knew they'd clean her up and wheel her down to the east porch, where they would have cake and ice cream. Her two sons and daughter from Florida would be there along with their children and their children's children. She loved them all, but couldn't remember their names or who belonged to whom. She'd smile for the camera holding the newest addition to the family. That was fine, but "let's not take too long doing it." The only thing she wanted for her birthday was a bottle of single malt. Hopefully Glenfiddich. Her son Arthur would take care of that. He always did. He was a good boy. He cared.

"There is another way. A peaceful way. You don't have to continue suffering."

Those words wouldn't leave her alone.

At first, she couldn't imagine doing something like that, but she was coming around with Lucille gone and the constant pain. Her mind was still good, but the ever-present torment of her body affected her thoughts. She didn't have anything to hope for in this world. She believed in John 3:16-17. She had no doubts. She believed God would understand.

For the most part, she had a good life, except for that one time. After 68 years, he still haunted her. He still tormented her. She didn't expect to see him in heaven.

The next day, after her birthday party. One more night of torture, and it would all be over. She was told it would be painless. Well, even if it were painful, so what.

Tommy Two Pockets
And the Posse of the Marsh

She knew she wasn't the only one. She heard the talk. She saw the results. She heard,

"Well, at least they're not in pain anymore."

That sounded pretty good to her.

"There is another way. A peaceful way. You don't have to continue suffering."

Tomorrow would be a day of goodbyes. No one would know she was saying farewell, but that was alright. She had her own birthday party planned. She wanted to share that bottle of single malt while saying goodbye to Mabel and Julio and her champion from long ago, Tommy Two Pockets.

Chapter 2 - The Home

"Mr. Tupoc.....Mr. Tupoc.....I know you hear me, Mr. Tupoc."

Agnes put her hand on his shoulder and gave him a little shake.

"Come on, Mr. Tupoc, supper starts in 5 minutes. Meatloaf Wednesday, you don't want to miss it."

"Meatloaf Wednesday, what a shame it would be to miss that! I look forward to Meatloaf Wednesday as much as I do Tuna Tuesday or Macaroni Monday. Tell me, Agnes, what kinda critter do you think they found along the road this week for Meatloaf Wednesday? Hope the cat's safe. Do you think those powdered mashed potatoes will be warm this week or still frozen? Wouldn't want to melt that pad of Oleo. And how about those green peas and carrots? At least, I think they're carrots. Probably orange peels, for all I know. No, couldn't be that. I haven't seen an orange since I came to the "Happiest Place Your Money Can Buy." Great ad. Hey, I hear Harold Goodman kicked last night. What are my chances of getting his old seat next to Gertie Does? You know she's sweet on me?"

"Now, Mr. Tupoc, you know we have assigned seating for a reason."

"Well, what in God's name is that reason, Agnes? I've wanted to know for the last 3 years, and damned if I can find out."

"Mr. Tupoc, please. You know the rules about cursing."

He put his hand to his mouth, shrugged his shoulders, and looked around.

Tommy Two Pockets
And the Posse of the Marsh

"Oh shit, I forgot. Please tell me about those rules again."

"Mr. Tupoc, please. All the rules are in your handbook. You know perfectly well what it says about using foul language."

"Handbook, my ass. It makes the New York City phone book look like a flyer out of the Gazette. That damn thing is so big I can't even lift it. It sits there on my little desk, or whatever the hell that glued-together particle board is, and collects dust. Hey, that's where I can get some real potatoes. I'll plant 'em there."

"Oh Mr. Tupoc, you are incorrigible!"

"Probably. Are you sure you even know what that word means, Agnes? Was that the Reader's Digest word of the month? I'm proud of you for putting it in a sentence."

"Now, that is quite enough, Mr. Tupoc. There is no need to be abusive toward the staff. We're just here to try to help you."

"Well, while you're helping people, why don't you help yourself to cleaning Jimmy Cooper's ass before supper? I have a hell of a time trying to eat on Hamball Friday when he's got a full load in his drawers. Every Friday, same damn thing. I think it's the corn beef hash surprise we get for breakfast on Friday morning. Doesn't hit his bowels til about 5 in the afternoon, then flushes all the way through. And Hamball Friday is the only meal I truly enjoy during the week. Although I must admit, if they get a good burn on the Cheese Whiz they use on Cheese Sandwich Sabbath, I like that."

"Oh. Just get to the dining room, please."

Tommy Two Pockets
And the Posse of the Marsh

"Go ahead, Agnes, I don't mind following you. Reminds of when I worked at a pig,,,,"

"You don't want to finish that sentence, Tommy Two Pockets!"

"Ok, but I'm gonna think it."

Tommy joined his tablemates as the staff was handing out the trays.

"My compliments to the chef, Marcus. That fruit cocktail looks to die for."

"Yeah? Well, eat right up, Tommy. Do us all a favor."

"Ah, you just got your eye on my pillow from the New York World's Fair. Well, you can't have it, Marcus. It's in my will. Going to Mabel here."

Mabel smiled across the table at Tommy.

"Oooooh Tommy, I look forward to the day you die."

Mabel was sincere.

"Hey Marcus, where's the pad of Oleo for my potatoes?"

Marcus came around the table and looked down at his tray.

"It's there."

Tommy stuck his fork into the powdered mashed potato brick and lifted it up.

Tommy Two Pockets
And the Posse of the Marsh

"The Oleo must have evaporated."

"I'll inform the management."

"Yeah, Marcus, will you please tell the zookeepers they need to get the oven fixed? My potato brick is frozen."

"Do you hear anyone else complaining, Tommy?"

"How can they with all the zombie pills you guys feed 'em?"

"Yeah, whatever."

"Yeah, whatever. Go bother some other lucky resident Marcus."

"Two Pockets, if you're not going to eat those potatoes, can I have 'em?"

"Sure, Frank, catch."

He threw the potato brick across to Frank, who one handed it out of the air.

"Impressive catch Frank. Better be careful. You just got those dentures."

"I'll take it back to my room and put it on the register. It'll be my midnight snack."

Frank stuck the potato brick in his sweater pocket.

"Best of luck to ya, Frank. Geez, today's not Friday, is it?"

"No, look at your plate. it's Meatloaf Wednesday."

Tommy Two Pockets
And the Posse of the Marsh

"Oh, thanks, Frank. It just smells like Friday. Jimmy, what did you have for breakfast?"

"What's that?"

"What did you have for breakfast?"

"When?"

"Never mind."

He looked around the room and wondered why he was there. He was still pretty mobile and had control of his bodily functions. He was happy his talent for being a world-class smart ass hadn't left him. If not for Julio.........Julio.

"Well, have a wonderful evening, everyone. I'm outta here."

He heard a few grunts as he walked away from the table and went to the east porch to wait for Julio.

Chapter 3 - East Porch

For a ramshackle nursing home, the Mouillee Rest Home had a beautiful campus just outside the small town of Brownstown, Michigan overlooking the Lake Erie marshes. It sat high on a hill, which was extremely rare in the flatland that bordered the western basin of Lake Erie. Built in the early 1920s with funds donated by the bootlegging Lacavoli family, it set a higher standard for retirement home living in Michigan.

The Lacavoli cousins told the newspapers they wanted a place for their parents in their final days. However, no Lacavoli ever resided at the Mouillee Rest Home. Though it did come in handy for laundering money.

The facility eventually closed in 1938, after prohibition ended and the depression took hold. A group of investors bought the neglected campus in 1962 and spent just enough to bring it up to State code. In 1987, the Home was at maximum capacity, and there was a constant rumor among the residents that rates would go up because of the max cap. A second and frequently debated rumor was that a new residence building would be built on campus and block the view out to Lake Erie and the Detroit River.

From the east porch, residents could watch the big ships as they went by. Captain Dougherty, an old merchant marine captain, ran a ship-watching club for the residents. He would stand on the porch behind a maple lectern that a few of the fellas built for him in the woodshop. They had carved an anchor across the front and mounted an old bosun's bell on the side for him to ring when he wanted everyone's attention. With his binoculars, Captain's hat, ascot, and white Meerschaum pipe, he would talk about the different ships.

17

Tommy Two Pockets
And the Posse of the Marsh

He'd call the harbor master's office in Detroit and get the latest shipping schedule for the day. He posted this on the bulletin board marked with the boats he would talk about and the times they would pass by. He looked up the ship's details in his logs and passed that information to his dedicated following of about 30, who showed up with their treasured binoculars or tripod-mounted telescopes.

Captain Dougherty's genteel nature was in sharp contrast to his commanding presence even at 84 years old. No question was insignificant, and he showed great patience with those who asked the same question several times during one of his sessions. He lost his wife two years earlier to Alzheimer's and took pity on the dementia that attacked the residents without mercy.

One of Captain Dougherty's skills the residents greatly appreciated was his ability to keep Tommy's mouth under control with just a look. Something he learned to do with him 60 years earlier when he was a Chief Mate, and Tommy and Julio were deckhands on his boat. Tommy respected the Captain and envied him for keeping himself relevant.

"There you are. What did the doctor say?"

"Not good, Tommy, not good."

Julio shuffled over to Tommy, had a seat, took off his glasses, lifted his binoculars to the lake, and watched a regatta of Flying Scots approaching the windward turn.

"Watch 32. He'll cut behind 20's stern on the inside and steal his wind on the tack."

Tommy Two Pockets
And the Posse of the Marsh

"Nah, two bucks says 20 does an early tack and cuts him off."

"You're on, Two Pockets."

They watched through their binoculars as the play went down.

"No, don't let the main luff!"

"Ha, ha. Gotcha, Two Pockets!"

"Wait, not yet! That was an intentional stall! He's gonna let 32 fly by and then make a hard cut. Do it now! Do it now!"

"Didn't do it. That'll be a deuce, Two Pockets."

"Put it on my tab."

Julio pulled out a small notebook and licked the end of the stubby pencil he had in his shirt pocket.

"Alright, what's my total?"

"Let's see ... 2 plus 1,799 equals 1,801. You owe me 1,801 dollars, Two Pockets. I'll take it in small bills."

"I'll pay you at the end of the month."

"Yeah? What year?"

"2020. I'll have the cash then."

Julio did some calculating in his notebook.

Tommy Two Pockets
And the Posse of the Marsh

"That should work just fine. I'll be 109, and you'll be 110."

"Well, I plan to be around. I suggest you take better care of yourself if you want to collect."

"Yeah, I suppose."

"You didn't tell me what the doc said."

"That's right."

"What? Is it a big state secret or something? Did he tell you your pecker's gonna fall off?"

"Might be easier to control if it did. Hell, I haven't used it for its intended purpose since 1975."

"Yeah, right, Julio, you're still a virgin."

"Yeah, Fern Macke didn't think so."

"Fern Macke. In your dreams."

"Sweet dreams."

"Remember what happened to her?"

"Yeah, she ended up at Miss Nellie's 69 Red Light Club in Detroit and then married that Fricke kid in 32 or 33."

"Oh yeah, Forest. She had to be 7 or 8 years older than us. Huh."

"I liked her. Man, could she swear."

Tommy Two Pockets
And the Posse of the Marsh

"Yeah, she taught us a lot."

"So back to the $10,000 question."

"That would be funny if it wasn't so accurate."

"What do you mean, Julio?"

"Well, if I want to get my plumbing fixed, I gotta get my hands on some cash. Medicare will only cover so much."

"You need $10,000?"

"No, I need $2,100."

"How much do you have?"

"Right now, or what will I have after the social security check gets run through the home and they hand me the $32 that's left over?"

"So you don't have anything."

"Correct, but I can't complain. I get fed three times a day, and I got a bed in my own room."

Julio Garza never had much, to begin with. He was born in 1911 into a family that would eventually have 9 children before the 1918 Spanish Flu pandemic took five of his siblings, leaving him the youngest. Julio's mother pulled him through before succumbing to the disease herself. His father, Juan, worked in the Lake Erie commercial fisheries in one form or another and made just enough to get by. They lived in a small rundown three-bedroom bungalow behind Black's

Tommy Two Pockets
And the Posse of the Marsh

Fish House next to the Tupoc's. His father was fortunate to find work at Black's or on a fishing boat.

After his mother died, Julio was pretty much on his own. He was a runt and much smaller than all the kids in his rough neighborhood, but he was nevertheless lucky. He had Tommy Two Pockets.

As a grown man, Julio stood no more than five foot three and weighed around 110 lbs. at his heaviest. But that didn't stop him from joining the frequent fights he and Tommy found themselves in. He never married, though he had many girlfriends through the years. The responsibility of marriage just didn't interest him in the least.

His father died in 1925 when he got tangled in a gill net. He drowned before they could get to him.

Julio quit school two years earlier at 13 to work in the fish house cleaning fish 12 hours a day during the season. Off-season he would scrounge with Tommy.

In the winter following his father's death, he was the only one left in the house after his older brothers and one sister moved away. He could not afford the rent and slept in whatever shack he could find, on a boat in dry dock, or whatever ship he was on. Until he ended up at the Mouillee Rest Home, that was the height of his housing situation.

So when he said he can't complain because he got three meals a day and a bed in his own room, he meant it.

"Ding.......Ding.......Ding"

Tommy Two Pockets
And the Posse of the Marsh

"Ahoy mateys. If you look 20 degrees starboard, you will see the SS James P. Emerson belonging to the Grant Steamship Company. If you recall, I was Captain of this vessel from 1961 to 1970, prior to its conversion to an auto unloader. It is an ore boat, meaning we carried taconite pellets from the mines in Minnesota to be processed in the steel mills along the shores of the Great Lakes. One such steel mill sits just north of us, about 10 miles. Erie-Ontario Steel."

Captain Dougherty gave the dimensions of the boat, capacity, fuel consumption, draft, size of crew, and so on. He realized that other than a very few, he was talking to himself and delighted in any response he got from his audience. Many were hard of hearing or had no interest other than watching the ships as they passed. For most, it was a social event.

"Now, if you point your binoculars at the wheelhouse deck, that's the upper deck in the front of the boat, you will see something special."

"Where?"

"The front.....the highest deck Mrs. Russell."

"The front....highe.....Oh.... Oh.. I see it.... They're waving at us. Do you see that Marvella, the boys on that ship are waving at us?"

"Where? I don't see any boat."

"Oh Marvella, you're not even looking in the right direction."

"Tommy, would you help Marvella, please."

Tommy Two Pockets
And the Posse of the Marsh

"Aye aye, Cap."

"I arranged this with Captain Myers, so let's wave back at them. I know they will appreciate it as much as we do."

"Hey, Mabel, lift up your sweater and give 'em something to appreciate."

"Tommy, you stop that."

"Aye aye, Cap."

"Mrs. Russell, can you help Mabel? Oh no."

Too late. Mabel was standing up and shaking her fallen d cups. Most of the men started laughing as they could see the ship's crew pointing and laughing.

"Mabel.... Mabel....Come on dear, let's get you inside. Mr. Dougherty, if you can't control your group better than that, we may have to think about canceling future lectures."

"Now, now, dear Agnes. You know this is the highlight of the day for many of these people, including myself. Now, I want you to think long and hard before you make any decisions to discuss this with Ms. Haverhill. You will be doing us all a great disservice. I expect you to report to me at 1300 hours tomorrow when your shift starts and tell me that you are not going to do anything rash."

"Of course, Mr. Dougherty."

"That's Captain Dougherty, Agnes."

"Yes sir, Captain Dougherty. Now come on, Mabel."

Tommy Two Pockets
And the Posse of the Marsh

Agnes left, pushing Mabel along.

"Tommy."

"Aye, Cap."

"Don't ever do that again."

"Aye, Cap."

"Unless I'm standing in front of her. Drinks at 20 hundred hours?"

He raised his eyebrows up and down and winked.

"Aye Cap."

Chapter 4 - Rosie

Captain Dougherty had one of only a dozen of the deluxe suites in the independent living section of the Rest Home. It was decorated in black walnut paneling with deep blue tones. Pictures of the ships he served on and his crews and different ports of call tastefully hung on the walls. Maps of the Great Lakes, achievement plaques, and pictures with company and political dignitaries were also hung. Glass cabinets from his days on the lakes held nautical memorabilia. A Ramsden sextant, gimballed brass navigation compass, a well-used Weems and Plath Navigation set, 8-day ship's clock, and his most treasured item, the Marconi wireless transmitter he trained on at the Massachusetts Maritime Academy. This, along with numerous other trinkets and memorabilia, made Captain Dougherty's deluxe suite a maritime museum.

His balcony that overlooked Lake Erie and the marshes were why he settled on the Mouillee Rest Home. And that is where the five gathered.

"I do hereby call this meeting of the *Posse of the Marsh* to order. Your turn to bring the bottle, Mooch."

"Right here, Cap."

"Let's see what you brought. Oh, Grand Marnier. Good choice, Mooch."

Cap poured, and Mooch passed around the snifters.

"Julio, a toast, please."

"Ah, sure. Let's see. To Mabel."

Tommy Two Pockets
And the Posse of the Marsh

They all shouted.

"Here, here, to Mabel!"

"Tommy, did you know she'd do that?"

"I'll tell ya, Suds, Mabel's been like that since we were kids on Blacks Bay. Ain't that right, Julio?"

"So right, but she wasn't slutty or anything. No, she just liked to shock people, and she didn't fear anything or anybody."

"That's for sure. You know Cap, she was part of the original *Posse of the Marsh.*"

"I knew you had a few girls in it, but I didn't know Mabel was one of them."

"Tommy, tell them about that time Old Man Black's grandson came for a visit."

"Oh geez, Julio, it's a little long."

"Well, it ain't like we gotta be at work in the morning. Let's hear it."

"Ok, Suds. Is that alright, Cap?"

"By all means, Tommy, the floor is yours."

Tommy took a sip of his drink and lit his pipe, as did everyone else, though most had strict doctor's orders not to.

Tommy Two Pockets
And the Posse of the Marsh

"I believe it was the summer of 1921. We had formed the *Posse of the Marsh* a year earlier to deal with Lumpy Pies, but that's another story altogether. Anyway, most of the kids our age were spending the summer finding little odd jobs we could do to help out our families. It was also a way to get out of the house so we wouldn't have to deal with family troubles.

Well, Old Man Black had this grandson. What was his name, Julio?"

"Roosevelt."

"Oh yeah, Roosevelt. His Ma named him after Teddy. He would have been better off if they named him Teddy, but he got stuck with Roosevelt. Of course, being kids, we couldn't leave it alone."

"Hell, you can't leave anything alone now. What's being a kid got to do with it?"

"He's got a reputation to keep up as a world-class smart ass, Suds."

"Ain't that the truth."

"You guys wanna hear this or not?"

"Proceed, Tommy."

"Thanks, Cap."

"What was I saying?"

"Roosevelt."

Tommy Two Pockets
And the Posse of the Marsh

"Oh yeah. Well, anyway, this kid comes down from Detroit to spend a couple of weeks with the grandparents, and his name is Roosevelt. Roosevelt Burnside. So like I was saying, we had all kinds of fun with his name. Now Roosevelt was probably a year older than the rest of us and kind of a soft kid. I mean, he never had to worry about finding some work so he could eat, like the rest of us kids in the area. He didn't have to watch his backside every time he walked down the street, and he certainly didn't know how to put up with a bunch of crap. Of course, we gave him lessons in both regards.

Old Man Black was a swell guy and used to look out for us kids. If he knew we were hungry, he'd put some perch in the fryer and have us sit on the Fish House stoop while he handed out old sheets of newspapers rolled up in a cone with a couple of pieces of fried perch in it. I'll tell you what, that was the best fish we ever ate, ain't that right, Julio?"

"So right. Old Man Black was the best too."

"That he was. That he was. So Old Man Black told us his grandson was going to be with him for a few weeks and would we watch out for him and take him fishing and stuff. So we had a special meeting of the *Posse of the Marsh*, and it was unanimous. We'd take care of him if he wasn't a shit, and that's exactly what we told Old Man Black. I says.

> "Here's the skinny Mr. Black. If he ain't the shit. Well, we'll make sure he has a good time."

Old Man Black stood there, rolled a cigarette, and says to me:

> "And what if he is the shit?"

Tommy Two Pockets
And the Posse of the Marsh

I stood back, cocked my cap, put my thumbs in my belt loop, and looked up at him.

"Well, we'll be obliged to give him the shit," says I.

"Fair enough, Two Pockets. Might do him some good. Just don't kill him."

"The posse don't kill folks, Mr. Black."

"Well, that's good to hear."

Then we spit in our hands and shook on it.

I'll never forget the first time we met Roosevelt, and Julio beats me to the punch. Well, we made sure the *Posse of the Marsh* was there to greet him. Let's see. There was me and Julio, Mabel, Lumpy, Sonny, and who am I missing, Julio?"

"Dory and Lips."

"God, yes, how could I forget Lips. We called him that because he didn't have any. Made his beaver teeth stick out all the time. Couldn't call him Beaver either. His older brother already got that name."

"Like I was saying, Julio here beats me to the punch. Tell 'em, Julio."

"Ok. I says.

"Hey, Rosie."

Tommy Two Pockets
And the Posse of the Marsh

Well, he got all puffed up and made a fist and stuck it in front of my face and says. "You call me that again, midget, and I'll bust your nose."

Tell 'em what you did, Tommy."

"Well, I gives Lips the high sign, and he gets down on all fours behind him, and then I gives Julio the high sign, and he gives Rosie a push. He goes flat on his back, and I hops on him and pin his arms down. I slap him in the face, and I says.

> "If anybody gives anybody a busted nose, or a black eye, or a gut punch, or a nut crack, or a tit twist, or a cheek pinch, or anything else, it'll be me or one of the posse if I tells em to, see?"

> "You can't do this, my daddy's a CPA, and my grandfather will beat your bottom."

I slapped his face again.

> "Thanks, I forgot that one. Nobody gets their bottom beat less I says so, see?"

> "My daddy's a CPA; you better stop."

> "Know what a CPA is, Lumpy?"

> "Nope, don't care."

> "Lumpy don't care, and neither does I."

> "You're gonna care."

Tommy Two Pockets
And the Posse of the Marsh

"I doubt it. Look, here's the skinny Rosie."

"Don't call me Rosie."

"While you're here, that's your name. Now shut your piehole and listen up, Rosie. Old man Black says we're to look out for ya while you're here and take you fishing and stuff. I told him we would if you wasn't the shit, and if you was the shit, we'd give you the shit. Now Old Man Black says that's fine with him. Right, Julio?"

"So right."

"Now you wanna go fishing?"

"I want you to get off of me."

"You wanna go fishing?"

"Yes."

"Ok. Tomorrow morning at daybreak. There's a rowboat down that way at the end of the dock. Me and Julio and Mabel will meet you there."

"You want me to go fishing with a girl?"

"Grab her, Lumpy."

Mabel was ready to have at him.

"Hang on, Tommy, I have to go to the head. Mooch, why don't you make another pass with the bottle."

Tommy Two Pockets
And the Posse of the Marsh

"Aye aye, Cap."

All the current members of the *Posse of the Marsh* crewed at one time or another with Captain Dougherty, and they were all just as loyal today as they were on board the ships he captained.

"Anybody else need the head? No? Please proceed, Tommy. No, wait, wait, I almost forgot the caramel rolls. They're being kept warm in the oven. Suds, come help me out."

"Aye aye, Cap."

That morning Tommy and Julio absconded with a tray of caramel rolls sitting on a cart waiting to be taken into a Mouillee Rest Home monthly board meeting. They could do this because Suds and Mooch created a fake heated argument to distract the staff. Of course, it was a political discussion.

"Here we are, men. Coffee is on the way. Another victory for the *Posse of the Marsh!*"

They raised their glasses.

"*Posse of the Marsh!*"

"Carry on, Tommy."

"Aye aye, Cap."

"So the next morning here comes Rosie walking down the dock looking like he just walked out of the Sears catalog wearing a Sam Carter fishing hat, tweed jacket, tie, fishing vest, and knee-high rubber boots. Old Man Black stood there on the dock watching him, shaking his head. He knew his grandson was in for a rough day.

We sat in the boat in our rags and stared. And rags are exactly what they were. None of us had shoes, and the rope I had holding my ripped-up pants was the newest thing I had on. And I had that for a couple of years.

Well, he's carrying this bamboo fishing pole with a backlash special on it. You know, one of those gearless baitcasting reels that only God himself could use."

"Oh yeah? Let me tell you how my uncle taught me......"

"Hang on there, Suds. One story at a time. Tommy's got the floor."

"Aye aye, Cap."

"Tommy?"

"Ok. Where was I?"

"God's ability with a bait caster."

"Thanks, Mooch. Well, anyway, we all have eight foot of braided line with a #2 hook and a ½ ounce sinker Old Man Black gives us. We had cut some new willow branches the night before, and that's what we fish with. So Mabel, she says."

"You know how to use that thing, Rosie?"

"Don't call me that."

Tommy Two Pockets
And the Posse of the Marsh

"You know how to use that thing?"

"It's the latest available on the market. Very popular on the Au Sable."

"What the hell is the Au Sable, Rosie?"

"Don't call me that."

"What the hell is the Au Sable?"

"A river up North. Loaded with Brown and Rainbow Trout."

"What's a trout, Rosie?"

"Don't call me that."

"Ok, I'm asking you what a trout is, and I'm calling you Rosie. So is she, and so is Julio. Got it? Now answer the damn question."

Rosie gave me the stink eye and said.

"It is a very delicate and tasty fish."

"Ever hear of carp.........Rosie?"

"Don't.........no."

"Very delicate and tasty fish."

"Wonderful. Will we be catching carp?"

"Not if we can help it."

Tommy Two Pockets
And the Posse of the Marsh

"But you just said.......never mind. Can we go?"

Rosie went to the bow of the rowboat, sat with a smug look on his face, and pulled out a store-bought briar pipe. So we pulled ours out too. All handmade and seasoned."

"I still got mine. Right here."

"Yeah, Julio. You had the best one. Made out of black cherry, isn't it?"

"Yeah, and I...."

"Ah, let's stick to the story Tommy."

"Aye aye, Cap."

"So......oh yeah. So we pull out the rough-cut Durham tobacco we got out of the big jar at the general store, and Rosie starts packing his with this packaged stuff. Saint something or another."

"Julien. Saint Julien."

"Your memory's better than mine, Julio. But that's right. It really smelled good. Ours smelled like a mule fart. But we weren't about to ask him to try some of his fancy stuff. So we're all taking turns rowing the boat, including Mabel. She could row as good as any of us. But not fancy boy who says;

"The guides would always do that."

Well, I didn't want to argue with him because I didn't want to take the time to teach him. Anyway, we get out near the west

Tommy Two Pockets
And the Posse of the Marsh

end of the peninsula and head into a creek that takes us to a pond in the marsh. We figured we'd fish for panfish that day. You know, sunfish, rock bass, and Crappie. Maybe get lucky and run into a northern or a smallmouth bass. So we get there and throw out the anchor, and what's dufus do? He stands up in the front of the boat and gets ready to cast his line out.

"Hey genius, hold on a minute."

"What? Are the fish here or not?"

"Yeah, but a couple of things."

"What?"

"First thing. Sit your ass down. This ain't an ocean liner you know. You tip the boat; we're all going swimming. And second, you'll have a much better chance catching a fish if you put some bait on your line."

"Oh, right. I ah, was just checking out the gear."

"Right. Here catch."

I threw him a minnow, and he flinched and let it go overboard.

"Hey, careful, we don't have that many, and I don't want to have to seine for more."

"I got it, Two Pockets."

"Thanks, Julio."

37

Tommy Two Pockets
And the Posse of the Marsh

So Julio here put his bait on for him, then we all sat back for the big moment, and he didn't disappoint.

He reared back and caught Julio in the pants. Julio here just pulled out his toad sticker and cut it out. What was another hole anyway? So little Julio sits there and points the pocket knife at Rosie and says. Oh, you tell 'em, Julio."

Julio pointed his pipe at Mooch and said in his best Bogart voice

"You do that again, and I'll use your nuts for bait, see?"

"Relax, Mooch, he didn't mean it."

"Aye aye, Cap."

Mooch wasn't too sure.

"Proceed, Tommy."

"Aye aye, Cap."

"So he tries again. This time, as expected, the line turns into a rat's nest, and his cast goes six feet into the water. Well, he's in the front of the boat. We know he's got a mess, but he acts like nothing happened, and he just sits there. We all start to snicker when all of a sudden, all hell breaks loose. The tip of his rod goes right to the water. We all go to the bow to watch this four-foot sturgeon about to pull Rosie in.

"What do I do? Help! What do I do?"

"Let Two Pockets have it."

Tommy Two Pockets
And the Posse of the Marsh

"No. My fish, I'll do it."

"Ok then, Rosie, do what I tell you. Hold the rod in front of the reel and keep the rod tip up, and we'll try to grab it as it goes by."

"Ok, ok."

"Hold it up!"

"I am!"

"No, you're not! Like this!"

"Let go. I'll do it!"

"Ok. Don't let it go under the boat; it'll cut the line. Hold it up!"

Well, he didn't hold it up, and the sturgeon went under the boat along with Rosie's fancy gear.

"This is your fault. You didn't help me."

"Hey, wait a minute, knucklehead, I tried. You wouldn't let me."

So he keeps yelling at me. I'm getting pissed and just about ready to slap the bejesus out of him when we hear Mabel scream out.

"Look what I got! Look what I got!"

Tommy Two Pockets
And the Posse of the Marsh

She had reached down and pulled Rosie's rod out of the water. The cork handle let it float. Well, she pulls up on the rod, and the sturgeon is still there. She gets it by the side of the boat, and me and Julio manage to get it in.

"Nice fish Mabel!"

"Good catch."

"Thanks, boys. Ain't it a swell fish!"

"The cat's meow, Mabel.

"And how!"

"Hey, wait a minute, that's my fish."

We all stopped and looked at Rosie standing in the front of the boat.

"It's Mabel's fish."

"That's not fair. I caught it."

"You lost it, Rosie. I caught it."

"You give me that fish."

Well, Julio grabs the head, and Mabel grabs the tail.

"One, two....."

"Hey wait a minute!"

Rosie raised his hands to protect himself.

40

Tommy Two Pockets
And the Posse of the Marsh

"Three!"

The fish flew through the air, slapped Rosie in the head, and knocked his Sam Carter hat in the water as the fish flew to its freedom. We all about busted a gut while he was up front wiping the fish slime off his face. Finally, he said:

"Give me my rod back."

"Fat chance."

"That's my rod. I paid for it with my allowance."

"What in tarnation is an allowance?"

"Give it back."

"It's hers, Rosie. Finders keepers, losers weepers."

Mabel looked at it with the line all tangled.

"Looks like you wasted your money, Rosie. You want it, Julio?"

"No."

"Two Pockets?"

"No."

"Ok, Rosie, you want it, go get it."

She threw it as far as she could in the water.

41

Tommy Two Pockets
And the Posse of the Marsh

"Are you crazy? I'll get you for this!"

"Now this, I'm going to keep."

We looked at Julio in the back of the boat wearing the Sam Carter hat.

"Now wait a minute, you can't take my Sam Carter hat."

"I didn't take it. I found it. Here you can have my old one."

He threw his old ratty newspaper boy's cap at him. Rosie knew he couldn't win, so he sat in the front of the boat while we commenced fishing.

"We brought a willow pole for you to use, Rosie."

He didn't answer and turned around, facing the bow. We parked ourselves right over a submerged brush pile and started pulling in slab crappie, and pretty soon, we heard a "Pop" and "Fizz." There Rosie is drinking a Vernor's Ginger Ale he pulled out of his fish creel. Now, none of us had ever tasted a soda pop let alone a Vernor's. He sat looking at us with a smug look on his face.

"Wanna taste."

"Yeah."

"Apologize."

"Your Mother's knickers."

Tommy Two Pockets
And the Posse of the Marsh

"Dry up."

"What a sap."

"I'll let you have a drink, Mabel."

"Really?"

"Show me your tits."

"She just turned 12, no Mabel!!"

Too late. She pulled her ragged shirt up and down as fast as you could blink an eye. She held out her hand for the bottle.

"No."

"She showed ya, now give it up."

"No. She doesn't have any tits."

"Of course not, you idiot."

"No tits, no drink."

"You better give me a drink of that."

"No."

Now Rosie starts teasing her. He stands up and holds out the bottle, and as she reaches for it, he pulls it back. After the third time, Mabel charges him. One hand on his neck and one hand on the neck of the bottle. As he went over the boat's port side, she watched him struggling to stay afloat with all the weight from his outfit. She took a long pull on the Vernor.

> "That's the ticket. Give her a try, boys!"

Rosie finally found the side of the boat while we sat drinking his pop and puffing on our pipes with his St. Julien tobacco. After about half an hour, we pulled Rosie back in the boat, rowed over, and picked up his rod floating in the water. When we got back to the dock, I made Julio give back his hat."

"I liked that hat."

"Soon as we pull up to the dock. Rosie starts crying and telling Old Man Black, we did this, and we did that, and what was he gonna do about it. All this time, Old Man Black is rolling a cigarette and finally says to Rosie."

> "Shut up Roooosie. Now get up to the house. You kids got yourself a nice bunch of fish. Clean em, and I'll fry em up for ya. Thanks for teaching my grandson how to fish. Will you take him out again?"

> "Anytime, Mr. Black. Our pleasure."

"Thank you for that interesting story, Tommy and Julio. Now for the business portion of our meeting. Gentlemen, I understand that Friday night's movie is *"The Cave People of Mars*." Now while I'm sure this great motion picture from 1957 holds some fond memories of the second feature at the drive-in movies, most if not all of the residents will just watch in a catatonic state and sleep through this as well. My question to this group is, do we find this acceptable? Are we willing to accept that they continue to deny our petition for John Wayne or Audrey Hepburn?"

"I really liked her in *African Queen.*"

"You're the only one, Suds."

"Now wait a minute, Mooch. Didn't she receive an academy award or something for that picture?"

"It was Kate. And Bogie won the academy award."

"*Kiss me Kate?* I didn't know she was in that. And you say Bogie won for *Kiss Me Kate*? Well, he should have."

"Just leave it alone, Mooch."

"Aye aye, Cap."

"Now as I was saying, are we willing to continue to accept that thcy will only show movics givcn to them from the drive-in when it shut down 15 years ago?"

"I gotta movie we can show."

"Ok, Mooch. Is it appropriate for all ages? Mental ages that is?"

"No."

"Perfect. Two Pockets, I am putting you in charge of getting this movie in the queue."

"Aye aye, Cap."

Tommy Two Pockets
And the Posse of the Marsh

"That concludes the business meeting. Any further topics of discussion?"

"Yeah, Cap. I propose that because tomorrow is Bran Flake Thursday, we meet at Dolly's Pancake House for breakfast."

"Right, Suds, just like every week. All in favor, say aye."

"Aye Cap."

"Unanimous."

"Meeting adjourned."

"Hey Tommy, I'm having a little trouble with my legs right now. I think I'll skip Dolly's this week. That's kind of a long walk for me."

Tommy looked at Julio.

"Are you telling me everything the Doc said?"

"Sure."

"Look, I'll borrow a wheelchair out front, and I'll push you. It's only three blocks."

"You don't have to do that."

"That's right, and don't forget it. Besides, it's downhill both ways."

"Ha, ha."

Chapter 5 - Ms. Haverhill

"Mr. Tupoc......Mr. Tupoc."

"Let's go, Julio. We're almost to the door."

"Mr. Tupoc, you stop right there. I know you can hear me. Hank, stop them."

"Oh gosh, don't sic Renta-Hank on me."

Hank blocked their way.

"Mr. Tupoc, I need you and Mr. Garza to come back here so we can talk."

"Your legs are younger than mine. You come here."

"Hank."

"All right, don't get your shorts in a bunch."

They slowly made their way back to Ms. Haverhill, who was standing by the door to her office.

"Taking a field trip Mizzz....Haverhill?"

"What?"

"Well, you're at least 15 feet outside your office. Why are we so honored to see you out and about with the inmates?"

"Inmates? We do not refer to the residents of the Mouillee Rest Home as inmates."

Tommy Two Pockets
And the Posse of the Marsh

"Better issue a memo to the rest of the zookeepers because that's exactly what they call us. And with good reason, I might add."

"Mr. Tupoc, I don't intend to let you disparage my staff."

"Disparage, now that's a good word to use, isn't it, Julio?"

"So right."

"You been in the Reader's Digest too Mizzz..... Haverhill. Agnes had a good one yesterday. She said I was incorrigible. Am I incorrigible Julio."

"So right."

"Is this a staff improvement program you got going Mizzzz......"

"That is quite enough, Mr. Tupoc. I have a couple of things to talk to you about."

"Ok. I have a couple of things I want to talk to you about."

By now, Ms. Haverhill was in her full "had it up to here" look. Julio wondered what she would look like if she smiled, but decided not any better. He'd never seen her in anything other than a navy-blue business suit. The tight skirt was three inches above her knees and showed a pair of thigh scrapers that struggled into her complaining pantyhose every morning. The jacket needed another foot of material to be buttoned around her puffy white blouse. Her ratted jet-black hair hadn't changed since she graduated from high school in 1957, except for the predominant gray roots. Julio was impressed with the maker of her size 4 narrow high heels

Tommy Two Pockets
And the Posse of the Marsh

that held in her size 6 double wides. He figured that's why she took such short steps. Or maybe it was the tight skirt. He didn't know and didn't want to watch her anyway.

"First, Mr. Tupoc, we are getting a lot of complaints about your cursing."

"No shit. Tell me who the hell it was, and I'll put a stop to it."

"It's about you, Mr. Tupoc. You need to clean up your language and stop swearing."

"Hell, I don't swear, do I, Julio?"

"So right."

Tommy crossed his arms and nodded his head up and down in defiance.

"Don't push it, Two Pockets."

"I didn't know you considered me a friend Mizzzz....Haverhill, Can I call you Grizelda?"

"No, you may not, and why do you think I think we're friends."

"'Cause only my friends call me Two Pockets, and if you want to get that personal with me Griz, then I'm calling you Grizelda. By the way, what a lovely first name. Your parents must have had visions of you stirring a cauldron. Weren't too far off the mark, were they, Julio?"

"So right."

Tommy Two Pockets
And the Posse of the Marsh

"Mr. Tupoc! Put a cork in it."

"No. I don't think I will."

Ms. Haverhill looked at the floor, took a deep breath, and they could hear her whisper.

"6, 7, 8, 9, 10."

"There is something else, Mr. Tupoc. There is a matter of some missing caramel rolls."

"Why are you telling me?"

"Because I believe you took a tray of caramel rolls intended for our monthly board meeting yesterday morning."

"What did they look like?"

"You know exactly what they looked like."

"Tell me what they looked like, and I'll tell you if I've seen them."

"I don't know what they looked like because you took them."

"Now, how do you know I took them?"

"Because you were seen with a tray covered by a white cloth heading toward the deluxe suite wing."

"Was this the same person that told you I was swearing? Hell, you can't believe them. Right, Julio?"

"So right."

Tommy Two Pockets
And the Posse of the Marsh

"Mr. Tupoc, you know what the handbook says about stealing?"

"Right Griz. Better gets another memo to your staff because they don't know it's against the rules to steal."

"Mr. Tupoc! I will not stand here while you accuse this wonderful staff of stealing."

"There's a chair, Griz. Have a seat, and I'll clue you in."

"No, I will not sit down. If you are going to accuse my staff of stealing, you damn well better have some proof."

"Did she just swear Julio?"

"So right."

"You want proof, Griz? Then I suggest you put on your tennis shoes and go for a walk this afternoon at 1 o'clock after the shift change. Go stand on the west porch and watch the staff walk home with supper. The other day I saw one of your underworked custodians walk out of here with a crate of apples. Do you know when the last time I saw a piece of fresh fruit was, Griz?"

"Mr. Tup......"

Tommy had on a full head of steam and was in Ms. Haverhill's space, making her slowly step back.

"Shut your piehole and listen to me. I was here for about a year, and I remember the Doctor congratulating me on keeping my weight down. I came back and noticed something. The only fat people I saw were the staff."

51

Tommy Two Pockets
And the Posse of the Marsh

"That's because we feed you a balanced nutritious meal."

"My ass, It's because you're starving these people. Last night my powdered mashed potatoes were frozen. The meatloaf for the never-ending Meatloaf Wednesday was made of duck butts. Right, Julio?"

"So right."

"I get one decent meal a week, and you just stopped us from getting that. We were heading to Dolly's."

"I approved of the menus myself. There is nothing wrong with the food we serve."

"That must have been a tough job because in the three years I've been here, we have the exact same damn thing week after miserable week."

"So, are you looking for some variety Mr. Tupoc?"

"Julio?"

"So right."

"What I am looking for is variety, quality, bigger portions, seconds, real warm potatoes, cold milk, hot coffee, clean plates, real fresh fruit, and a place to eat that doesn't smell like the men's head at Tiger Stadium."

"So right."

"As you know fully well, Mr. Tupoc, we have a formal complaint system set up through the suggestion box."

Tommy Two Pockets
And the Posse of the Marsh

"Oh, I'm glad you brought that up. Come here, look. It's right here. Look."

Tommy opened it up, and it was stuffed full. He pulled the suggestions and shuffled through them.

"Look, Griz. Here's one I put in December of last year. What's that, almost 6 months ago? Here's another one. And here's another one. Look at this one. Submitted April 1982 by Captain Ethan Dougherty. That's five years ago. YOU NEVER LOOK AT THE FRIGGIN' THING!"

With that, he grabbed the letters and threw them in the air.

"Security!......Security!"

"I don't know what you do all day in that office besides watch your soap operas while you're drinking those White Russians!"

"Security!"

"Oh yeah, we know all about it, you worthless cu......
Hank had Tommy in a shoulder pinch and pushed him down into a wheelchair.

"Leave him alone!"

Julio raised his cane and was just about to give "Renta" Hank a night in the hospital when he was grabbed from behind.

"Take Mr. Tupoc to his room and have nurse Fletcher sedate him. Him too."

Tommy Two Pockets
And the Posse of the Marsh

"Leave Julio alone. He didn't do anything."

"That's ok, Two Pockets. I'll take a double."

Chapter 6 - Lumpy

They left Tommy sitting in his chair looking out the window at the weeping willow tree down by the marsh pond. The benzodiazepine they gave him was kicking in full force, and he was starting to enjoy the trance-like feeling it gave him. The willow tree was gently swaying, and he could hear its seductive call through the open window. He watched as a fox, half-hidden in the reeds, waited for a mallard to come around the other side of the tree. The fox was quick, had the duck by the neck, and shook it.

*****

"Stop! Leave him alone."

He turned and backhanded Julio.

"Stop it. Lumpy, you're going to kill him."

Tommy felt himself running to the willow as Lumpy shook Sonny by the neck. He watched as Julio got up and Lumpy hit him again. Tommy grabbed a stick. As he got to Lumpy, broke it across his back, knocking him down."

"Awwww........I'll kill you, Two Pockets."

"Come on, Lumpy. Give it a try!"

Tommy stood there with his fists up, ready for battle. He knew if Lumpy got hold of him, there was a good chance he would kill him. Lumpy was a little older than Tommy and almost twice his size. He had a thick neck and head to match. His hair was cut in a bowl style and made him look

Tommy Two Pockets
And the Posse of the Marsh

like a picture Tommy once saw of the *Hunchback of Notre Dame*. He had broad, powerful shoulders and heavy hands from all the cordwood he had to split daily. At 12 years old, he looked at a life that would wear down his body before its time.

His father, Otis Pies, was a woodcutter supplying cordwood to all the locals. He was an ill-tempered man who maintained a monopoly on the cordwood business in the area. Whether they liked it or not, everyone bought firewood from Pies Cords. He knew how much they would need through the winter, and by God, that was what they were going to buy.

"And don't let me find you cutting your own wood. Taking food out of my family's mouth."

That was the message he gave to everyone, and everyone knew he would back it up. Pepper Ernst challenged him by cutting up a tree that fell behind his house and was splitting the wood when Otis came up behind him and slapped him on both ears. Now Pepper was no weenie, having served with Teddy Roosevelt's Rough Riders and winning the 1st Volunteer Cavalry heavyweight boxing Championship. Pepper dropped the ax and turned around.

"Otis, what in the hell is wrong with you?"

"Taking food out of my family's mouth."

"You're out of your mind Otis."

Otis wound up to give Pepper a haymaker, but Pepper sidestepped him and punched him on the side of the face as he went by. As Otis was recovering, Pepper went into the classical boxing stance of the time, which was a mistake

Tommy Two Pockets
And the Posse of the Marsh

against a brawler like Otis. He charged Pepper's legs, took him down, sat on him, and proceeded to change his looks. With Pepper lying on the ground moaning, Otis took the ax and started splitting the wood. When he was done, he stood over Pepper and said that'll be 90 cents. Pepper just moaned, so Otis reached into Pepper's pocket, found a dollar, and put it in his pocket. He pulled a dime from his vest and threw it on the ground next to Pepper. His business was steady after that.

"Run, Sonny! Julio.........NO!"

Julio was on Lumpy's back and biting his ear. Lumpy started spinning around and finally reached back and pulled Julio over his back and slammed him on the ground. He lifted one of his heavy work boots to stomp on Julio when Tommy slammed into his off-balance body. As Lumpy went down, Tommy rolled off him, jumped up, and grabbed Julio's hand.

"Let's go!"

They ran about 30 yards, stopped, and mooned Lumpy sitting on the ground holding his bleeding ear.

"You're dead! Both of ya! I'll get you!"

They ran behind one of the many fishing shacks that lined Black's Bay, where they met up with Sonny. They sat behind some old crates taking inventory of their injuries. Sonny's neck was starting to show bruises though they were hard to see through all the layers of dirt. Julio had a black eye, a lump on his head, and blood all around his mouth.

"Lumpy gave me something."

Tommy Two Pockets
And the Posse of the Marsh

"What did he give you besides a black eye?"

"This."

He opened his mouth and pulled out a ½ inch by ¼ inch piece of Lumpy's ear. They rolled on the ground laughing.

"He will kill you, Julio."

"So right."

"What were you guys doing to piss him off?"

"Breathing."

"What?"

"Breathing. He came up to me and said I had to stop breathing his air, so he grabs my neck and starts shaking me. Isn't that right, Julio?"

"So right."

"He's lost it. We gotta do something about him."

"What are we gonna do against that ape, Two Pockets?"

"I don't know."

"I know."

"Well, spit it out, Sonny."

"Posse."

Tommy Two Pockets
And the Posse of the Marsh

"What? Posse?"

"We'll form a posse?"

"What's a posse, Sonny?"

"Remember Hickory Bob shot up the saloon, and forms themselves this posse."

"Oh yeah, *Denver Dan and the Wild Mustangs of the High Plains.* Yeah, I remember that. You gave me that pocket book to read."

"Yeah, and I want it back, Julio."

"Two Pockets has it."

"I forgot to read it. Anyway, tell me about this posse."

"Well, you see, any time somebody does something bad, the town folks gets together and forms themselves this posse. Then they goes and gets 'em. See?"

"What do they do once they get him?"

"They strings him up."

Julio pantomimed, wrapping a rope around his neck and choking.

"Are you saying we should hang Lumpy?"

"No, but a bunch of us should get together, form a posse and do something to him. We needs to punish him and tell him there will be more if he doesn't leave us alone."

59

Tommy Two Pockets
And the Posse of the Marsh

"Sonny, for a dumb ass, you're pretty smart."

"Thanks, Two Pockets.......I think."

"That might work. Ok, who do we want in this posse besides us?"

"Mabel."

"Yeah, Mabel, for sure."

"Mabel will want Dory."

"Yeah, Dory's good. She's smart."

"Lips. We gotta have Lips."

"Yeah, he picks on Lips more than anybody."

"Lips will want to hang him."

"We'll have to tell him it's a last resort. Ok, let's meet at sundown in Kramer's shack. Julio, you tell the girls. Sonny tells Lips."

Chapter 7 - Cap Visit

Tommy smelt a pipe, lifted an eyelid, and looked at Captain Dougherty sitting next to him.

"You really did it this time, Two Pockets."

"What time is it?"

"Oh, a little after seven. I figured you'd missed supper, so I made a sandwich for you. Hope you like pimento loaf and Swiss cheese."

"Mustard?"

"Honey mustard. Brought us a couple of Stroh's too."

"You're the best, Cap."

"I dropped one off for Julio too. Gotta look out for my men. Gotta look out for the Posse."

Cap popped the top on both beers and handed one to Tommy. As Tommy ate the sandwich, they sat and watched the sun go behind the willow tree, creating dancing shadows on the lawn.

"Griz is really pissed. She came to my apartment looking for me."

"She must be pissed if she left her sanctuary."

"Oh, she is. I thought she was going to have the big one right there. She was telling me how you went off on her about the food around here. She also told me you're pushing your luck and that I better get you under control, or you'll be told to leave."

"Sucks."

"I agree. Now Tommy, I have to admit, I don't pay too much attention to the food. I mean, I go down, sometimes I eat, and sometimes I don't and well. Being a boat captain, you get used to guys complaining about this and that and, of course, the food."

"Food on your ship was always good, Cap. The best."

"Thanks Tommy. I knew it was, so I guess I just learned to tune out the complaints and not pay too much attention. I'm sorry to say that I also tuned out the complaints here. Quite frankly, I'm happy. I have the added advantage of an apartment with an efficiency kitchen, and I supplement my meals with whatever I want."

"Cap, we don't have that luxury."

"I know Tommy. I'm sorry for being so blind. Look, what I'm trying to say is. I have the resources to help my friends out. If you're hungry and need something to eat, come see me. I can........."

"Stop Cap. No disrespect, but that ain't it at all. I mean, I appreciate what you're saying, but this conversation shouldn't even be happening. We shouldn't have to put up with being fed like we're in some third-world country. Griz treats us like shit, and something needs to be done about it!"

"Did I offend you, Tommy?"

Tommy Two Pockets
And the Posse of the Marsh

"You've always been great to Julio and me. There's nothing you could do to offend me. Like I say, you're the best Cap. But you can see what's happening here. You're a smart guy. What can we do?"

"Well, we need to think about this. Let's get the *Posse of the Marsh* together, tomorrow ten hundred hours, my place. I'll get the word out. Oh, and if Mabel was a member of the original Posse, shouldn't she be now?"

"As far as I'm concerned, you are for life once you're a member. But I haven't had her come because she didn't mate with you."

"Oh, there's still that possibility. Ha..Ha.."

"I meant be a mate on one of your ships."

"I know, I know. She's in the Posse. Bring her on board."

"Aye aye, Cap."

The Captain stood up and put his hand on Tommy's shoulder.

"Well, I've got to be going. I've got a date tonight with Gertie Does. She's coming to my apartment to watch the 9 o'clock movie. *"From Here to Eternity."*

"Muscling in on my girl, huh?"

"You know the saying. You snooze, you lose. Now go back to sleep."

"Aye aye, Cap. Have a good time."

Chapter 8 - The Posse

Tommy went to his tiny bathroom and got ready for bed. He wasn't quite ready to lie down yet, so he sat by the window and listened as the day prepared to go to night in the marsh.

He felt lucky to have this room with a great view. He didn't know much about music, but he envisioned God conducting the marsh orchestra. The wind would play the piano on the willow tree and the marsh reeds, bullfrogs the bass section, spring peepers the woodwinds, swans, geese, and ducks the brass section. To his ear, it all worked together and made music only he could hear. Music that calmed him as it had throughout his life. At that moment, with all the frustration he felt with his situation, he was content.

*****

He listened and watched the sunset before opening the door of Kramer's shack. A candle was lit and sitting on a crate. Everyone was there.

"Good, everyone is here. Did you tell them your idea, Sonny?"

"Sure did Two Pockets."

"Well, the first thing we gotta talk about is who's gonna lead this here posse."

"You."

"Ok, Mabel. Anyone else wants to lead it?"

They all sat shaking their heads and mumbling "no," "nope."

Tommy Two Pockets
And the Posse of the Marsh

"Alright, so I'm the leader."

"We need a name."

"What needs a name, Mabel?"

"The posse. We can't just call ourselves a posse. We need a name. We can't just call ourselves a posse or the posse."

"Mabel's right. We need a name."

For the next 10 minutes, they went through a litany of names; Black's Posse, Peninsula Posse, Our Posse, Posse to Hang Lumpy, Mossy Posse, Poop Posse, Snot a Posse.......and on and on.

"No Lips, we ain't calling it the Split Lip Posse."

"Why not? Don't we want to give Lumpy a split lip? Yeah, that's the punishment the Split Lip Posse will dish out, see?"

"You just want that name, so people will think it's your posse. Right, Julio?"

"So right."

"Sonny, what are you shaking your head about?"

"Well, there was another of those pocket books I read. *Denver Dan and the Posse of the Pecos.*"

"You want to call us the *Posse of the Pecos*? What's a Pecos."

"Wait, Two Pockets. He's onto something."

Tommy Two Pockets
And the Posse of the Marsh

"Why's that Dory?"

"Where do we live? What's around us?"

"Air. *Posse of the Air.* I don't think so."

"Shut it, Lips, before I step on your neck."

"Ok, Dory! Geesh!

"Come on, think."

"Water?"

"Trees?"

"Ducks?"

"Marsh?"

"The marsh. Yeah, the marsh."

"*The Posse of the Marsh.*"

"I think you got it, Dory. Everybody good with that?"

Everybody said good except,

"So right."

"We needs a warrant."

"A what?"

"A warrant."

Tommy Two Pockets
And the Posse of the Marsh

"Ok, Sonny, is this something you read in a Denver Dan nickel book?"

"They costs a dime, and yes, we need a warrant that tells about all the things Lumpy's done to us 'ns."

"What did he say, Dory?"

"We need a list of his crimes."

"We ain't got that much paper or time."

"Don't worry about it, Two Pockets. Let me write something up and go from there."

"Ok. Julio, you got that pocket notebook and pencil? Give it to Dory."

"So right."

"I gotta take a leak."

They all did, including Mabel, who squatted on the other side of the big oak the boys were using.

"All done. Here ya go Two Pockets."

"Read it, Dory."

"For spitting, hitting..."

"Wait a minute; it needs to say, "We are hereby charging you with the following crimes against us all.""

Tommy Two Pockets
And the Posse of the Marsh

"Ok, put that in there, Dory. Anything else Sonny?"

"I'm sure I'll think of something."

"I'm sure you will."

"We are hereby charging you with the following crimes against the *Posse of the Marsh.*"

"Hey, that's not how it goes."

"Stuff it Sonny. Go on, Dory."

"Ok. For spitting, hitting, gouging, kicking, slobbering, titty twisting, knee popping, banana stealing, ear smacking, goober chunking, hair pulling, underwear toading, choking, stealing, gut-busting, and being an all-around son of a bitch pain in the ass with a bad haircut. We....
What do I say next, Sonny?"

"We do hereby sentence you to whatever we are going to do to you."

"Ok, put that in, Dory. Now, what do we do with it?"

"We reads it to him before we do whatever we're going to do to him."

"Sounds fair. Ok, what are we gonna do to him?"

"Hang him."

"As a last resort, Lips. I don't think the *Posse of the Marsh* should go around killing people."

Tommy Two Pockets
And the Posse of the Marsh

"How bout everybody holds him, and I bust his lip?"

"No, he'll kill us all. I don't think the six of us can take him."

"I know."

"What's that, Dory?"

She reached in her back pocket and pulled out her slingshot.

"At twenty yards, I can hit his boogers."

They all reached in their back pockets and pulled out their rabbit killers—an essential weapon for any hungry kid.

"Ok. Here's what we do. We go to Pie's clearing, where he's splitting firewood in the morning while his old man is out making deliveries. We make a circle around him, far enough away that we dodge an axe or a piece of wood if he throws it. Then Dory reads....."

"No, you're the leader; you read the warrant. That's your job."

"Alright, Sonny. I'll read it. Then we commence to letting him have it. Now no stones bigger than the end of your middle finger. We want to hurt him but not kill him. But have a couple of rabbit killers with ya, just in case. No head shots. Just go for the body."

"What about the nuts? He's always trying to hit me in the nuts."

"Ok, Lips. Nuts are fair game. Meet here at seven-thirty tomorrow morning."

Tommy Two Pockets
And the Posse of the Marsh

"I don't got no watch."

"Don't be a knucklehead, Sonny. What's the church do every ½ hour."

"Oh yeah."

"Alright, see you in the morning."

Chapter 9 - Tommy

Tommy and Julio stayed behind.

"I brought you a blanket. I'll bring you something to eat in the morning."

"Thanks."

"How long is he here for?"

"Tonight."

"Same shit?"

"Yeah."

"Alright. I'll see you in the morning, Tommy."

"Thanks Julio."

"So right."

Tommy's dad Tony came in that morning for one of his irregular monthly visits. He was a merchant sailor who took the long routes. Tommy didn't really know him and tried to avoid him if he could. He wasn't mean to him, but Tommy didn't trust someone who never shut their yap, and that was Tony. But his total conversation with Tommy lasted as long as it took Tony to say.

"You being a good kid, Tommy?"

"Tommy's a good kid, Tony. Don't cause no trouble."

Tommy Two Pockets
And the Posse of the Marsh

"That's good, Gladys. Yeah Gladys, I hear the Ford plant they're building in Dearborn is hiring. I'm thinking I'll get me a job there and get off the ships. Be around more often. Would you like that, Tommy?"

"Oh, sure he'd like that, Tony."

Tommy heard this every month and hoped it wasn't true. Tommy was an only child due to some difficulties during his delivery. Gladys gave birth at home with help from her neighbor Lupee Garza. Tony was gone that long day, which was probably a good thing.

During the season, Gladys worked at Black's Fish House during the day. She sat on the back stoop in the evening, drinking the Mackinaw Mash she bought behind the general store. Winters were rough on Gladys, trying to depend on Tony's undependability. Sometimes she would disappear for a few days leaving Tommy on his own. She would have enough money for food, rent, and more Mackinaw Mash when she came back.

After supper, Tommy slipped out the back door as they pulled out the mash. He knew it would be an evening of drinking and thumping on the thin wall between their bedrooms. He wouldn't be missed.

Tommy's needs were never considered, and he was treated like he was on his own, which he essentially was. His mattress on the floor was one he found being thrown away after a flood. In fact, half of the furniture in the house was a result of his flood scrounging. He had no shoes, and in the winter, he wore rubber boots he found outside the fish house. He cut them down to resemble shoes and made triple-thick socks from old flour bags he found. He actually found it

Tommy Two Pockets
And the Posse of the Marsh

quite comfortable and warm, so he was satisfied. Any clothes Tommy had were from the St. Henry's quarterly thrift sale, and the choice was limited for boys. Father McMurphy tried to set aside anything he thought Tommy could use.

"Two Pockets, come here, come here, come here."

Father McMurphy quickly said as his whole body showed the excitement of his find. He took Tommy behind the table where Sister Marguerite was sitting, collecting money. To their faces, they were called Father Mac and Sister Mags, and they loved it. One of the best unkept secrets was that they lived in the Parish as husband and wife. Nobody cared or dared challenge it. They were of vital importance in the community, and everyone loved them.

"Look at this, Two Pockets."

He held up a blue cotton shirt.

"Look, look, look, it's got two pockets. The sleeves were a bit ragged, so Sister Mags turned it into a short-sleeve shirt. Now, there were a couple of holes that she mended that were here somewhere. Oh well, I can't find them. What do you think, Two Pockets?"

Tommy learned how to be a good horse trader, so he didn't want to tip his hand. He took a step back, cocked his hat to the side, and rubbed his chin.

"You say it has two holes in it, Father Mac?"

Father Mac knew the game and was delighted to play along.

73

Tommy Two Pockets
And the Posse of the Marsh

"No. It had two holes. Like I said, Mags, I mean Sister Mags, did a dandy job mending it."

"I suppose, but still...... hmmmmm.......Well I can't be standing here all-day squabbling over necessaries. What are you asking for this here, mended shirt, Father Mac?"

"Well, Two Pockets, let's see. This is a nice item, and I know of probably ½ a dozen boys that would want this shirt, but I'll tell you what I'll do. How does three cents sound?"

"Sounds like somebody else will be wearing this here shirt. But........... I guess I'd be willing to help you out and go a penny. And I got cash on the barrelhead, Father Mac."

"I just don't know that I can do that, Two Pockets. But for you, I can make it two cents."

"Weelllllll........Ok, you got a deal.'

They spat on their hands and shook.

"Oh..... you made a good deal there, Two Pockets. A real good deal."

Tommy started to dig the two pennies from his pocket.

"Two Pockets. I have another little matter I need to talk to you about. You know that Superior Plum tree around the corner of the Parish garage."

"Sure."

"Well, that darn tree is overloaded with plums this year, and the fallen ones are making a mess. I haven't had time to clean them up with the thrift sale and all. I wondered if you would do me a favor and clean up around that tree. It's a two-cent job, and to help stop that mess from getting any worse, go ahead and take down the ripe ones you can reach from the ground."

"Really. What do you want me to do with the ones I pick?"

"Oh, I don't care. There's more there than I can use. Just leave the ones that are higher up. Now you'll find two-bushel baskets and a wheelbarrow just inside the garage door. Just be sure to bring everything back when you're done."

Tommy put away his tough-guy act and wiped a couple of tears away.

"Gee Father Mac. You're the best."

Tommy gave him and Sister Mags a hug before running off to the plum tree. Father Mac yelled after him.

"See you at Mass Two Pockets!!"

Father Mac knew that several families would benefit from Tommy's generosity with the plums.

People liked Tommy and would go out of their way to say hello, slip him an occasional apple, or find some meaningless chore to let him earn a piece of pie or a bowl of homemade ice cream. They knew he had a hard edge and a smart mouth, but they generally liked his quick wit and defense of weaker kids. The best thing Tommy had going for him was respect. People reserved that kind of respect for someone they admired, and Tommy was admired.

Tommy Two Pockets
And the Posse of the Marsh

They knew they could depend on him. If someone had to move because they couldn't pay the rent, Tommy was there. If one of the elderly needed help hauling groceries, Tommy was there. If someone lost their dog or a cat was up a tree, or there was damage from a storm, or someone died, Tommy was always there.

He was ten years old when the flood hit. As the water was rising, he organized kids in the area to haul small pallets they commandeered from outside Black's Fish House. They went from house to house to get their valuables above the soon-to-be foot-high water. When Old Man Black saw what they were doing, he pulled a fish cart out of his building and helped them load the pallets himself. It was a long two days, and people remembered Tommy Two Pockets.

Tommy took the blanket up to the small loft and settled into the old sofa cushions and pillow Mrs. Kramer stored there. She knew the kids used the shed for a clubhouse and learned that sometimes one of them would need a safe place to spend the night. Tommy found an apple on the pillow. Mrs. Kramer knew Tony was home.

Tommy sat there in the dim light coming in from the loft window. He ate the apple and smiled. He liked living on Black's Bay.

Chapter 10 - Breakfast

He slept well that night and dreamed of being in Old Man Black's rowboat with Julio catching perch. When he woke, he wondered about the rowboat and reflected on the adventures he and Julio and the *Posse of the Marsh* had in it.

He took a long shower and prepared for the day. When he got to the dining room, he poured a cup of coffee out of the big urn. He took a sip, walked a few feet, then stopped. He smelled the coffee, turned around, looked at the urn, and took another sip.

"Hey Roberta, what happened to this coffee? Where's the beaver piss we usually get?"

"That's the way we were told to make it this morning. Got a problem? Talk to somebody that cares."

"No, no. It's good. Real good."

"Well, glad you like it."

He went over to the table, greeted everyone, and sat down.

"What's that smell?"

"What smell, Two Pockets? I don't smell anything."

"I don't either, Frank. That's just it."

"Hm. I guess you're right. It smells, well, I don't know?"

"Clean?"

Tommy Two Pockets
And the Posse of the Marsh

"By golly, it does. Got kind of an orange lemony aroma. Not too strong, but very pleasant. It reminds me of resting on a hammock under a Bougainvillea tree in Boca Raton in May. Waves gently rolling into shore. Watching lovely young ladies heading to the beach with their blankets and sun hats. Tango music drifts in from the Tiki at the Surf Hotel. Sipping on a Mojito."

"You do have a way with words, Frank. I feel ready to flag down a cabana boy for a sissy drink. But no, here's Raymond with our corned beef hash surprise?.........What? Where's the corned beef? French toast? Three slices?"

"Is that real butter?"

"Scrambled eggs with cheese? Yes, that's cheddar cheese. Oh my goodness."

Mabel put her finger in the syrup and tasted it.

"That's the real deal!"

"Look, Orange slices! And Orange juice!"

"Anyone got some Vodka?"

Everybody was looking around the table and at each other's plates. The chatter around the room went up several decibels. People were giggling as they dug in.

"Oh my, there's cinnamon on the French toast, and look how thick it is!"

"What's the special occasion?

Tommy Two Pockets
And the Posse of the Marsh

"Did they hire a new chef?"

"Where's the corned beef? It's Friday, and I was looking forward to my corned beef."

"You look forward to it, Jimmy, because it flushes you out."

"No Tommy. A guy my age don't like change."

"Jimmy, just try it. I think you'll like it."

"Oh, I don't think I will, but I guess I have to eat something."

After several bites, Tommy said.

"Pretty bad huh Jimmy?"

"What's that?"

"Pretty bad?"

"What? This is great. Eat up, Two Pockets. I think you'll like it more than that crap they usually give us on Friday."

Tommy hadn't touched his food yet and was looking around the room, watching the ravenous seniors devour their breakfast.

"Aren't you going to eat Two Pockets? After all, this is 'cause of you."

"I'm gonna eat it, Raymond, but what's shakin'?"

Tommy Two Pockets
And the Posse of the Marsh

"All I can tell you is, you must have really pissed off the Griz. She was in the kitchen this morning at 6 o'clock yelling and cussing and saying Two Pockets this and Two Pockets that."

"She must've forgotten about the swearing rules."

"I don't know, but she can put together combinations of words that I have never heard before. Something about a bastard ass shitbrain turd bucket: I think she might have been referring to you. Well, we were all enjoying the education, but then she starts in on us for making the same menu she put out four years ago. Claimed she didn't know we were still making the same menu and said that was supposed to be for a start and as an example and why weren't we being creative and shit like that. Well, we all look at each other and finally Thelma, you know Thelma? Big gal, don't take no shit, no prisoners? Well, she gets right in Griz's face and says,

"Tell me something Mizzzzz...... Haverhill, how did you find your way down here to the kitchen, because I've been here for 11 years, and this is the first time I've seen you down here. In fact, this is the first time I've ever seen you. You want something changed, all you gots to do is let us know. Just waddle your ass down here to the dungeon, and we'll be more than happy to do whatever the hell you want! And while you're at it, we needs some better ventilation down here."

"I'll look into it. Just make a good breakfast this morning and submit a new menu to me by the end of the day. And somebody clean the dining room. It smells like a chamber pot."

She looked at Thelma.

Tommy Two Pockets
And the Posse of the Marsh

"What's your name anyway?"

"Thelma. Thelma Jones. You can call me Mizzzzz..... Jones"
"Are you in charge down here?"

"No, that's the trouble Mizzzzz.....Haverhill. Nobody's in charge. Not since Bonnie retired when you started here 4 years ago. We all does our own thing."

"From now on, Ms. Jones, you are in charge."

"Do I gets more money?"

"Yes."

"How much?"

Then the Griz whispers in Thelma's ear, and Thelma turns around smiling and says.

"Come on. We gots us some cooking to do!"

Tommy started eating and wondered what price he would pay for this.

"Something wrong, Two Pockets?"

"No Mabel, I'm fine. Why?"

"I've known you all my life, and when you ain't talking somethings wrong."

"Eat your eggs."

Chapter 11 - Lips

Tommy caught up to Mabel after they left the dining room.

"What do you have going at 10?"

"A.M. I'm getting on my private jet to go to Paris. P.M. I'll be doing the tango with Sean Connery at the Chameleon Club."

"Tell that s.o.b.; he still owes Tommy Two Pockets 10 bucks."

"I'll be sure to do that."

"Well this a.m. I need you to go to Cap's suite."

"What for?"

"*Posse of the Marsh.*"

"I'm in."

"You know where it is?"

"Of course."

She winked and walked away.

Captain Dougherty had doughnuts and coffee out for everyone.

"Can I take this for later, Cap? That was a hell of a breakfast."

"By all means, Suds, help yourself."

Tommy Two Pockets
And the Posse of the Marsh

"Aye aye, Cap."

"Well, today we have a new member of the *Posse of the Marsh.*"

"Stuff it in your old lady's knickers, Captain. I've been a member of the Posse for 67 years!"

"My apologies, Mabel. That was very insensitive of me."

"Yeah, I was ready to crack your nuts."

"And with good reason. Can I say welcome back?"

"I'll take that."

"Then welcome back, Mabel, to the *Posse of the Marsh.*"

She raised her hand to puff the back of her hair and looked around the room with her nose in the air.

"My pleasha, I'm shua."

"Alright then, let's get down to the reason I've called you here. I'm sure you all have a busy day ahead. Someone wake Mooch."

"Huh, oh sorry, Cap."

"That's quite alright, Mooch. That breakfast probably put half the residents to sleep by now. Anyway, before I tell you why I called this special meeting, this morning my nephew Ralph, you all know him, right? Ralph Randazzo? Reporter for the Herald? Well, last evening, he came up with something he thought I should see. An obituary that ran over the Michigan

Tommy Two Pockets
And the Posse of the Marsh

AP Wire. It caught his eye because this gentleman was born at Black's Bay. Then he remembered the name from an old article his grandfather wrote back in the early 20s about when you were kids in the *Posse of the Marsh.*

"I remember that article, Cap. Who are you talking about?"

"We all knew him. He was a mate on my ships. Let me read it."

"Leonard "Lips" LaRue, 78, passed away on May 29, 1987, in Black's Bay, Michigan. Leonard was born March 6, 1909, to Larry and Minnie LaRue at Black's Bay. Leonard proudly joined the Navy on December 8th, 1941, to help defend his country. He served aboard the USS Battleship North Carolina, where Leonard received a purple heart and the Silver Star during the battle of the Eastern Solomon Islands. Leonard was credited with bringing down two enemy planes after being wounded and refusing to leave his post. As a result, Leonard used a cane for the rest of his life.

In 1945 Leonard met and married Linny (Rasmussen), who passed away in 1974 after 29 years of marriage. Together they had three children Leonard (Eve) LaRue Jr., Blacks Bay, Minnie (Buck) Baynes, Traverse City, Sister Mary Claire, Little Sisters of the Poor, People's Republic of the Congo. And six grandchildren. Millie, Tilly, Willy, Mona, Andy, and Lisa. After the War, Leonard worked as an Engineers Mate aboard ships that served in the Great Lakes. From 1970 until his retirement in 1980, he was a boat mechanic at the Fricke Island Marina. He will always be remembered for his infectious laugh and a big smile.

The Anderson Funeral Home is handling funeral arrangements. Visitation will be at St. Henry's Catholic

Tommy Two Pockets
And the Posse of the Marsh

Church, Black's Bay, Friday, June 12th, from 6:00 to 9:00. Funeral Mass will be Saturday, June 13th at 1:00."

The room was silent.

"Tommy, you ok?"

"Aye aye, Cap....No Cap. Can you give me a minute?"

"Yes, let's all take about 15 minutes."

"Thanks, Cap."

Tommy went out to the balcony and thought about Lips, and the day the *Posse of the Marsh* went after Lumpy with their warrant. Once Lips got a thought or a direction in his head, it was hell getting him to change. He supposed that's why he kept shooting after he was wounded. He was determined. That's probably why he was such a good mechanic. He was certainly determined when he showed up that morning.

Chapter 12 - The Rescue

"What the hell are you doing with that clothesline Lips?"

"Stuff it Sonny."

"Two Pockets said we weren't hanging him."

"He said last resort."

"You can't hang him with that. It'll snap."

"I'll double it up and snap his neck."

"Well, you can't bring it."

"I'm bringing it."

"Tell him he can't bring it, Two Pockets."

"Bring it, Lips."

"What? You said we wasn't gonna hang him. If you're gonna hang him I ain't going. I don't want to end up in no reform school."

"I don't wanna end up in no reform school. Boo hoo hoo. Ya weenie."

"Shut up Mabel."

"No, you shut up Sonny."

Tommy Two Pockets
And the Posse of the Marsh

"Everybody shut up. Bring the rope. We can use it for our escape plan. We'll tie it low between two trees, and if things go wrong, we'll jump over it, and Lumpy will fall on his ass."

Lips stuck out his tongue at Sonny.

They made their way through the woods to Pies clearing when they heard Otis Pies yelling.

"What are you supposed to do with the ax when you're done?"

"Oil it and put it away."

"Oil it and put it away. Did you do that? Answer me, boy! Did you do that?"

"No."

"What did you do?"

"Left it in the block."

"Left it in the block and what happened last night."

"It rained."

"It rained. And now what do we have?"

"Rust."

"RUST! WE HAVE A RUSTY AX! I OUGHTA CHOP OFF YOUR DAMN HANDS, YOU STUPID PIECE OF SHIT! NOW BEND OVER!"

Tommy Two Pockets
And the Posse of the Marsh

"No Pa, please!"

"I SAID BEND OVER NOW, OR BY GOD, I'LL USE THE AX INSTEAD."

"No, please......please."

They came to the edge of the clearing as Lumpy, with no shirt and his pants pulled down around his ankles, bent over the chopping block. They watched as Otis put all his weight behind the first strike with the razor strap.

CRACK

"OWWWWW.......uh....uh....uhhhh."

"YOU CRY, AND IT"LL BE WORSE!"

CRACK

"OWWWW,,,,,,,,,,,,Owwwww........."

" SHUT UP BOY."

Tommy stood there shaking.

CRACK

"OWWWW.........owwww...."

CRACK

Tommy found the biggest rock he had in his pocket and walked into the clearing.

Tommy Two Pockets
And the Posse of the Marsh

CRACK

"OWWWWW........."

He raised his slingshot, pulled back, and let it fly. The rock bounced off of Otis's head and staggered him. He turned around, and Tommy let him have it again, This time on the cheek. By then, the rest of the Posse joined him and were pelting Otis with rocks.

"Aim for his head and use your big rocks!"

"LUMPY, PULL YOUR PANTS UP AND RUN!"

Lumpy looked dazed.

"Go help him, Lips."

Lips ran around Otis, helped Lumpy pull his pants up, and grabbed his shirt.

"Come on, Lumpy, come with me."

As Lips took him back to the woods, Otis reached into his back pocket and pulled out a small pistol.

"HE'S GOT A GUN! RUN!!!"

Otis fired two rounds in the air and then started chasing the Posse. They jumped over the rope. Otis didn't and fired a shot as he was going down. Dory fell. Tommy ran back, picked up a thick stick, hit Otis in the head as he was starting to get up, and grabbed the gun. Sonny and Lumpy already had Dory and were carrying her. When they were deep in the woods, Tommy faintly heard Otis yell.

Tommy Two Pockets
And the Posse of the Marsh

"I'll kill you, Two Pockets."

Chapter 13 - Pallbearers

"Tommy. Come on, let's go. Cap wants to start. What's the matter? Lips?"

"Yeah. Ever think about those days in Blacks Bay, Julio?"

"Do you mean do I ever think about Lips and Lumpy and.............Otis?"

"Yeah. The whole *Posse of the Marsh* thing?"

"Every day."

"Me too."

"When did you say the funeral was Cap?"

"The 13th, Mabel."

"Wonder why they're waiting so long?"

"Yeah, that's two weeks away."

"Well, I received a phone call about an hour ago from his son Leonard Jr. He said it would take them that long to get his sister back from Africa. But he called because he wondered if we would consider being honorary pallbearers."

"Do what Cap? And who are we?"

"You Tommy, Suds, Mooch, Julio, and myself."

"What's an honorary pallbearer mean?"

Tommy Two Pockets
And the Posse of the Marsh

"Leonard Jr. first asked me if we would be pallbearers, and I told him that none of us, except maybe you, Tommy, were in any shape to be lifting a casket."

"Now wait a minute there, Cap. I used to be able to deadlift 350 lbs."

"Used to is the key there, Suds."

"I can lift you over my head, Two Pockets. Here let me show you."

Suds went over to Tommy, who was sitting in a chair, prepared his stance, and motioned for Tommy to stand up.

"Go ahead, Two Pockets, let him lift ya. Should we call for an ambulance first or after you break yourself trying, Suds?"

"Very funny Mooch. I know I couldn't lift you. I couldn't get my arms around you."

"Have a seat, Suds. You'll just hurt yourself. Come on, John (his real name). We just celebrated your 81-birthday last month. You know better."

Suds looked around the room, pursed his lips together, and shook his head back and forth.

"I know I'm old Cap, and I probably couldn't lift him an inch off the ground, but..........you could at least let me try."

"I get it, Suds."

"Do ya Tommy?"

Tommy Two Pockets
And the Posse of the Marsh

"Yeah."

Tommy looked at him, slowly stood up, and turned around. Tommy, at six feet, was about four inches taller than Suds but weighed about the same at 180 lbs. Suds came up behind him, slightly squatted, and put his arms around Tommy.

"Tommy, please don't let him do this."

"I have to Cap. Sorry."

Suds lifted Tommy's feet off the ground and then turned full circle before putting him back down.

Everybody cheered and congratulated him, but tears were pouring down his face as he walked over to Cap. With his bottom lip shaking, he pointed his finger at Cap and said;

"I'm still a man, Cap. Now you call that boy of his, and you tell him that John "Suds" Sutherland will be a pallbearer for his buddy Lips' funeral. Now you tell him that!"

"Tell him Julio Xavier Garza will be a pallbearer too."

Cap started to say something but thought better of it.

"You too, Two Pockets? Mooch?

"Yep."

"Yep."

"Hey, Lips was my pal too, Cap. What about me?"

Tommy Two Pockets
And the Posse of the Marsh

"I'll tell him Mabel."

Cap looked around and smiled with pride at his group of friends.

"Well, today's meeting went in a different direction than I originally planned. I called you here so we could discuss the food situation, but it appears that Two Pockets has solved that problem, given this morning's breakfast."

"You really think so, Cap? I bet they go right back to the slop they feed us."

"Now, let's not be so negative, Mooch. Let's at least give them a chance."

"Yeah, well, I ain't holding my breath. I think they did that just to get Two Pockets off their back."

"Could be Mooch. Could be."

Chapter 14 - Lunch

Tommy took his time getting back to his room, thinking about Lips and the food situation at the home. He found a note in his mail basket next to his door when he got back.

Mr. Tupoc,

Please stop by my office after lunch. I need to talk with you.

Thank You,
Sissy Pervitch LCSW

"Great," he thought. "The Griz wants me to get counseling."

When he sat down at the table for lunch, Mabel complained about her leaky faucet.

"I've told housekeeping every day for the last two weeks. Yeah yeah, they say. We've talked to maintenance, they say. I'm going nuts, I say. We're very sorry, they say. I'm gonna kill somebody, I say. Have a nice day, they say."

"Who ya gonna kill Mabel?"

"I thought I'd start with you, Jimmy, and work my way around the table."

"Could you do it in my sleep? That's how I've always wanted to go."

"Pillow on the head, ok?"

Tommy Two Pockets
And the Posse of the Marsh

"No. Takes too long. Wouldn't happen to have a gun, would you? One right in the heart. I wouldn't want to mess my face up for the viewing."

"All I gots a shotgun, but maybe I can get a slug for it."

"That'll be just fine, Mabel. When do you think we can do this?"

Suddenly, she realized Jimmy was serious.

"Oh, Jimmy dear. What's the matter?"

Jimmy's once rugged good looks had left him long ago. A grey, sagging face with weepy eyes took its place. He chewed his lip and hesitated before finally saying.

"I'm 89 next week, Mabel. Lived longer than I ever expected. Longer than I ever wanted. I was an ironworker. Wasn't afraid of nothing. I walked the beams of half the skyscrapers in Detroit. I put the top cap on the Penobscot Building in '28. Walked my last beam in '69. I was 71 years old. Damn, my hip stopped me, or I would've kept going. But now, I don't know. Now I can hardly walk. Can't hardly hold a toothbrush. Can't remember where I put my damn cane when it's in my hand. Nurses changing my damn diaper. Wiping my ass. Hell, I'm a man, Mabel!"

HIs bottom lip was shaking as she reached over and grabbed his arthritic hand.

"Of course, you are, dear. Of course, you are."

Tommy Two Pockets
And the Posse of the Marsh

It broke Mabel's heart to have these conversations. Jimmy wasn't unique. Tommy wondered how long before he felt the same way. He knew it wasn't far off.

Raymond started passing out the trays.

"What the hell, Raymond?"

Single slice bologna sandwiches on thin white bread, with a skim of mustard. A canned pear half, a cup of coleslaw, two fake Oreo cookies, and a carton of lukewarm milk.

"I thought I was dreaming this morning."

"I'll tell you what happened, Two Pockets. The Griz called Thelma up to her office. You know none of us's ever been in there. Thelma says it was like walking into something you'd see in the movies. Big desk, two sofas, big console TV. Shit, there's even a fireplace in there and a wet bar. I told her she was playing with us. She says no."

"So, what did she want?"

"I guess she started to yell at Thelma about the breakfast this morning. Said she'd spent two days' budget on one meal, and she'd bankrupt the place if she kept doing that. So you know Thelma. She says she gave it right back to her. And I believe her. She said she told the Griz that if she ever talked to her like that again, to hell with the job and she'd turn Griz into a resident."

"No shit. What'd the Griz do?"

"Thelma says she went over to the bar and made them both drinks."

97

Tommy Two Pockets
And the Posse of the Marsh

"Was it a White Russian?"

"I don't know, but she said it was a white coffee drink with a kick."

"Yep, White Russian."

"So Thelma comes back all mellow and shit and says she and the Griz come to an understanding. Thelma says she made sure the Griz understood she'd cap her ass if she ever dissed her again."

"Dissed?"

"Disrespects. Anyway, we're supposed to go back to the old menu while they work out a new one."

"I guess this means Hamball Friday."

"That is a fact, Two Pockets. That is a fact."

"Great."

Chapter 15 - Miss Sissy

Tommy knocked on the door.

"Hello, Mr. Tupoc, please come in. Have a seat. Can I get you a cup of coffee? Just brewed it."

"Yes. Miss. Pervitch that would be nice."

"Please call me Miss Sissy or just Sissy if you want."

"Ok. Call me Tommy."

"Alright. Cream or sugar?"

"Black would be fine."

"Very good."

She placed the cup in front of him, sat behind her neat desk, and opened a file. While she was studying it, he couldn't help looking at her gentle and sincere face. Her short light blonde hair pushed back behind her ears.

"Is Pervitch your married name?"

"No, my maiden name."

"Hmm."

"What?"

"You know Miss Sissy. You kind of look like your grandpa."

"You knew my grandfather? Which one?"

Tommy Two Pockets
And the Posse of the Marsh

"Sonny. Isn't Sonny your Grandpa? I grew up with him on Black's Bay."

"You grew up with Grandpa Pervitch?"

"I did."

"He used to tell us stories of a posse and......Tommy Tupoc? Are you Tommy Two Pockets?"

"The same."

"Oh my."

Sissy got a big smile on her face and dabbed at her eyes.

"Oh, I loved Grandpa Pervitch. I used to sit on his lap, and he would tell me stories of the posse and things that happened on Black's Bay. What was the name of the Posse? I forgot."

"*Posse of the Marsh.* It was Sonny's idea. He got the idea from one of them dime novels. Denver Dan and........"

"*The Posse of the Pecos.*"

"How did you know that?"

"I have his Denver Dan books."

"You do? After all these years?"

"I have 10 of them. They're sitting on a shelf in my apartment. He gave them to me before he died."

Tommy Two Pockets
And the Posse of the Marsh

"1966. He died in 1966. Me, Julio, and Lumpy were casket bearers. Mabel was there too. Damn cancer."

"He called you a hero."

"Me?"

"He told me the story about the woodcutter probably, I don't know, ten times or so."

"Mmm... It was a different time back then. A hard time."

"Sounded like it. Do you ever see the other members of the posse?"

"Julio is here, and so is Mabel. Lumpy died about, let's see '79, so eight years ago. Dory's in Florida. We get a letter from her every Christmas. Mabel writes her and tells her how we're all doing. I just found out Lips died. Funeral's not for a couple of weeks."

"Lips? You mean Leonard LaRue, right?"

"You knew him?"

"Yes. I do some part time, temporary, when they need me, social work for another agency."

"So you saw him recently?"

"Yes. He'd been in the hospital, and I had to assure he had after-release care at home."

"What was he in the hospital for?"

Tommy Two Pockets
And the Posse of the Marsh

"I'm not allowed to say. I'm sorry."

"No. No, that's fine. I didn't even know he'd been sick. I haven't seen him since I moved here."

"Are you going to his funeral?"

"Planning on it."

She smiled at him, sat back, and took a long drink of her coffee.

"I bet my dad would like to talk to you. So would my brother Mickey. I'll have to let them know you're here."

"Is your dad Matt or Rudy? I haven't seen them since Sonny's funeral."

"Matt. My dad is Matt."

The phone started to ring, and Sissy answered it.

"I'll just be a minute."

"No problem."

While Sissy was on the phone, Tommy stood up and walked around the office. He looked at the degrees Sissy had on her walls. Bachelors, Eastern Michigan University. Masters, University of Michigan. Certificates of different endorsements. Family pictures and up in the corner was one of several kids. He took it down, held it, and started to cry.

"Tommy, are you alright?"

Tommy Two Pockets
And the Posse of the Marsh

"Yes, I just……..I'm sorry…..look….that's me. This is the *Posse of the Marsh*. I remember when that picture was taken. Reporter for the Monroe Gazette. Sissy, this is the only picture I've seen of me when I was a kid. That's Black's Fish House behind us. What?"

Tommy held the picture away from him to get a better focus.

"Sissy do you happen to have a magnifying glass?"

"I think I do. What is it?"

"I'll tell you in a minute."

She found the magnifying glass in her desk while Tommy sat back down, holding the black and white photo.

"Here you go Tommy."

He took it, his hand shaking.

"Can you help me here, Sissy? I'm having a little problem holding it steady."

"Of course."

She held it, and Tommy looked at the picture. He suddenly sat back, sucked in some air, and pulled his hankey out of his pocket.

"What? What did you see?"

"Do you see that lady sitting on the bench behind us? The one holding the coffee cup? That's my mother. And that's Mabel's mother next to her."

Tommy Two Pockets
And the Posse of the Marsh

"Oh....."

"I don't have a picture of her. As far as I know, she never had her picture taken."

Sissy sat in the chair next to him.

"Oh, Tommy. I am so sorry. I forgot that picture was up there."

"I don't know what to say. I'm....I guess I'm stunned. Do you have any plans for this picture?"

"Give it to you, but first, I want to make a copy."

"Can you do that?"

"Yes, of course."

"Can you make one for Julio and Mabel? And one for Dory in Florida?"

"Yes, I'll take it into the photo lab on my way home. I have a friend there that might be able to put a rush on it for me."

"Thank you Sissy. Do you know how Sonny got the picture?"

"No."

"Wait 'til I tell Julio and Mabel. By the way, what did you want to see me about?"

"After your little incident with Ms. Haverhill, I have to evaluate you to see if you could remain in the home."

Tommy Two Pockets
And the Posse of the Marsh

"And?"

"I'm going to recommend that I continue with a weekly evaluation, say around lunch, so that you can tell me about my Grandfather. Dolly's? I think I can put this on my expense account and let the Home pay for it."

"You're a sweet girl, Sissy."

"Well, I haven't always been that way."

"Yeah, right. Oh, one more thing. Kind of a heads up. You might want to check in on Jimmy Cooper. I think He's ready to check out."

"Thanks, Tommy, I'll do that."

Chapter 16 - Mabel

Knock. Knock. Knock.

"Go away!"

"Come on, Mabel, open up. I need to talk to you."

"Go away! My soap's on!"

"Mabel, this is very important. Now open up!"

He heard her grumbling.

"This better be good, Two Pockets. You've got three minutes. Commercials."

"Just listen."

"Better hurry up!"

"Then quit yacking."

"Ok shoot."

She turned around to see if her show was back on.

"Sonny's granddaughter works here."

She quickly turned back.

"Our Sonny? Sonny Pervitch?"

"Yep. Miss Sissy. You know her? The social worker?"

Tommy Two Pockets
And the Posse of the Marsh

"I know who she is, but I never made the connection."

"I had to go see her today and figured it out."

"Why did you have to?.......oh, never mind. Griz?"

"Yeah. Well anyway, we get to talking about Sonny and the *Posse of the Marsh*, and she gets a phone call. So, I walk around her office, and I see this picture on the wall, see?"

"Yeah yeah, a picture. Get on with it."

"If you don't interrupt me, I will!. So, I'm looking at this picture on the wall, and I realize it's us. The Posse."

"What?"

"It's a picture of all of us in front of Black's Fish House."

She turned off the TV.

"You're gonna miss your soap."

"Marvella will fill me in. I think she memorizes the damn thing."

"Remember the rules. No swearing."

"The hell. I remember that man taking our picture for the Gazette. Is it that picture?"

"Yeah, and there's something else. Your mom's in it. She's sitting behind us with my mom."

Tommy Two Pockets
And the Posse of the Marsh

Mabel sat down and pulled out the mysterious kleenex that appeared from nowhere.

"Can I see this picture?"

"She's making us copies."

"I don't have a picture of my mom."

"You will now."

"You've made my day Tommy Two Pockets. Was she wearing that old faded yellow dress?"

"Hard to say in a black and white picture, but probably."

Mabel stared off into the distance and started talking, lost in memory.

"I don't remember her wearing anything else for years. She smelled like the Fish House. I guess we all did. The smell was everywhere. I remember we'd take our bath on Saturday night, and after all of us kids were done, she'd just hop in the water wearing that dress and soap down, trying to get the stink out of it. She wanted it halfway presentable for Mass the next morning, but you remember Tommy, it never was. Our moms were both in the same boat, weren't they? A dad we hardly ever saw, a mom raising the kids on their own, and trying to earn a meager living at the Fish House. I remember I got my first job at fourteen, stocking shelves for Red Tompkins at the General Store. I saved my money and bought her a navy-blue cotton dress with lace around the collar and sleeves. Got it out of the Sears Catalog. I gave it to her for her 40th birthday."

Tommy Two Pockets
And the Posse of the Marsh

Tears streamed down Mabel's face. After a long pause, in a quiet voice she said,

"She got mad at me and I'll never forget what she said,

> "How could you get a notion that I needed fancies when we barely got enough money for food? I'm worried sick about rent this month and like every other month I haven't seen your father's check. This could've paid the rent. What were you thinking?"

She was right. What was I thinking? I remember being devastated and sitting in the corner and crying with my face in my hands. When I looked up, she was holding the dress and looking at herself in the tiny mirror we had hanging on the wall. And she smiled. She had the prettiest smile. One we never saw. She was a hard woman. She had to be. She came over and gave me a kiss on the head and said,

> "Now quit your crying. We won't talk about this no more and you won't be so foolish no more neither."

She wore that dress to Mass on Sunday and every Sunday for the next 10 years until.......until we buried her in it."

"I remember that dress. She was real particular about it. Carried a clothes brush in her purse and was always dusting herself off."

Then Mabel started sobbing.

"I'm sorry Mabel. What did I say?"

She gathered herself and said;

Tommy Two Pockets
And the Posse of the Marsh

"We put that brush in her casket."

They sat for a while, Tommy's hand on Mabel's shoulder while she finished crying.

"Funny thing Tommy. As tough as things were, I wouldn't change one thing about my childhood."

"Me neither. Did you realize how poor we were? I didn't. It just seemed normal to me. We were all poor back then."

"We were. I loved it on Black's Bay, but I don't know if I could've said that without you and Julio and Lumpy and the *Posse of the Marsh*."

"Yeah, we looked out for each other."

"We did, didn't we?"

Chapter 17 - Julio

"Thought I'd find you here."

"Hey, Two Pockets."

He told Julio about Sissy and the picture.

"I don't remember getting my picture taken as a kid."

"Yep. You had your cap turned to the right."

"That was the locked position."

"Yeah, I remember you were always in the locked position."

Julio's face got sad.

"What's the matter, Julio? Not feeling too good?"

Julio sat and looked out over the marsh pond. He was on a bench he and Tommy built when they first got to the home. It was in a hidden spot where you couldn't see the home, the road, or anything else except the marsh. They would occasionally bring a fishing pole down and catch some panfish, which they'd throw back because the kitchen wouldn't prepare it for them.

"State code." They said.

"Bullshit." They said back.

Julio came here to be with the occasional muskrat swimming by or the slap of a beaver tail in the distance. The co-ca-ree of red-winged blackbirds and deep-throated bullfrogs. The wind pushing the rushes back and forth, bringing peace, solitude, and sense to his world. He could forget about his body aches and the pain the memories of a hard life gave him. To just sit, listen, and smell. To empty his mind and relax his soul. It is where he wanted to be. It is where he needed to be, but his visits to the marsh pond were becoming less frequent. It was an overcast day, and they could feel the occasional sprinkle.

"Do you think we've led a good life, Tommy?"

"I guess so. Do you?"

"Wouldn't change a thing, although I wish I had kids. I think at this time in life a fella needs his kids. What about you Tommy? Wish you had contact with your kids?"

"Of course. I thought about hiring a P.I. again to find them, but I figured they could've done that if they wanted to find me. Let's see, Alex would be 50 and Trudy, I think 48."

"What about Meg? Do you miss Meg?"

"Every day."

The day Tommy left for WWII in 1942 was the last time he saw them. He never found out what happened during those chaotic days after being shipped home in '46. He couldn't figure out why she took the kids and left him. He thought they were happy. He thought she loved him.

He met her on the loading docks in Wyandotte, where she worked as a clerk at the Wyko Warehouse. He was waiting in line when she walked into the room and took his breath away. He was immediately smitten. She was tall, slender, and light on her feet as she floated around the room. As he was delivering the ship's documents to a shipping clerk, she came to the counter and asked him,

"You're from the Edmond Ross, aren't you?"

He just stared at her hazel eyes with his mouth open. She pushed back a strand of sun-bleached brown hair off her tanned face and looked up at him.

"Did you hear me?"

"What?"

"Did you hear me?"

"What?"

"Are you from the Edmond Ross?"

"Edmond Ross?"

"Yes, the Edmond Ross."

"No. My name is Tommy, not Ross."

"No, no. Are you with the boat, the Edmond Ross?"

"Oh. Ah.....yes I am."

"Good. Do you have the Lading Manifest from your stop in Cleveland?"

"The.....what?"

Tommy Two Pockets
And the Posse of the Marsh

"The Lading......Are you alright?"
"You're just so........."

She smiled at him, and that was the beginning of their short courtship.

They married in 1934, and three years later, Alex was born, followed by Trudy in 1939. They maintained a small apartment in Wyandotte, where Meg kept her part-time job at the warehouse while Tommy served as a deckhand on short-run assignments that allowed him to be home most weekends. Meg, an orphan, was not in touch with any distant relatives, so when Tommy came back from the war, he didn't know where to turn to find out where she might be. He was heartbroken, confused, and devastated. The seven years he had with Meg were the best and most stable time in his life.

"What's eating you, Julio?"

"Oh, I just keep falling apart. I'm wondering how I'm going to get back up the hill to the home."

"I'll help ya. Come on. We better get going. Those clouds are building up."

With Tommy on one side and the cane on the other, they slowly made their way back up the hill, stopping every few minutes. Halfway up, a gentle rain started.

"Remember what we used to do in rains like this, Tommy?"

"Get the soap."

Tommy Two Pockets
And the Posse of the Marsh

"Kind of fun watching all the folks around the Fish House take a shower in the rain. Remember we'd try to sneak a peek at Fern Macke behind those sheets they'd put up."

"Yeah, like that was really tough. A little wind and the show was on."

"What I wouldn't give to see Fern Macke again when a clothespin pops off."

"I just close my eyes when I wanna see her."

Chapter 18 - Abuse

Tommy decided he had enough time to go back to his room and close his eyes for a bit. He set his alarm so he wouldn't miss Hamball Friday and sat down in his easy chair. He thought about the picture he saw that day and started thinking about what led up to that moment. Eventually, he heard Otis yelling.

*****

"I'll kill you, Two Pockets."

Tommy caught up to Lumpy and Sonny carrying Dory.

"I'm shot, Two Pockets. He shot me in the ass. Am I going to die? Will I, Two Pockets? I'm only 11 years old. I can't die yet."

"No, you're not going to die Dory, but you might not want to sit down for a while."

"Is he coming?"

"No, and I've got his gun."

It was a .28 caliber revolver. More of a noisemaker than anything, but it could still do some damage from short range.

"Father Mac. Take her to Father Mac. He'll know what to do."

Old Man Black came out on the stoop as they passed the Fish House.

"What's wrong with Dory? Is that blood?"

116

Tommy Two Pockets
And the Posse of the Marsh

"She's been shot. We're taking her to Father Mac."

"Shot? How? Where?"

They were well past the Fish House, and Tommy yelled back.

"In the ass by Otis."

"Otis Pies?"

"Yes."

"Dory's father is in the fish house. I'll tell him, then go find the constable."

Tommy was too far away at that point to hear him.

They ran into the parsonage.

"Father Mac! Sister Mags!"

They both came running out of the small office.

"What happened?"

"Dory's been shot in the a........the butt."

"Oh my! Bring her into the kitchen and lay her on the table. Sonny, you run to the general store and have them call Doc Landrith."

"Yes, Sister Mags."

"Mac, take these boys out of here. I have to stop this bleeding. You stay Mabel; you can help me."

Tommy Two Pockets
And the Posse of the Marsh

"Yes, Sister Mags."

"Julio, you go find her parents."

"I think her pa already knows, Father Mac."

"Go find her mother then."

"Yes, Father Mac."

"Alright, let's leave the women to take care of Dory."

They told Father Mac what happened when Dory's dad, Gus Perkins, came charging in the door. He smelled like the hull of a fishing boat because that's where he had been. He grabbed Lumpy by the throat and pushed him into a wall.

"You shot my daughter!"

His arm was back, ready to hit him, when Father Mac put his arms around him, picked him up, and held him in the air.

"It wasn't him Gus. Ask the boys. They'll tell you it wasn't Lumpy. It was his father, Otis. He did it after the kids stopped Otis from beating Lumpy."

Father Mac let him down.

"Go see your daughter."

Gus continued to glare at Lumpy as he went to the kitchen.

"Lumpy, let me see your back."

Tommy Two Pockets
And the Posse of the Marsh

Lumpy pulled up his shirt and turned around. His back was bleeding and heavily scarred.

"Undo your pants."

Father Mac pulled down his pants enough to see that the cuts and scarring were there.

"Sweet Mother Mary."

"Tommy, look in that cabinet over there. There should be a can of Germolene salve halfway down on the left. Bring it here. Now Lumpy, I'm going to get a couple of blankets. I want you to strip down and lay on your stomach over on the sofa. Let's see if a little salve will help you out."

Father Mac sat in a chair next to him and started putting the stinging salve on Lumpy, but Lumpy just bit his lip and took it. The cuts and scars went from his shoulders to the back of his legs. Even though Father Mac saw all kinds of carnage in the field hospitals in France, this shook him to the core and made his blood boil. He knew many of the children in his parish were severely beaten, though he never saw anything like this. He was the child of an abusive alcoholic father, but his punishments paled in comparison. He prayed as he applied the salve and wondered what could bring a man to do this to his son - his only child.

Otis Pies and Lumpy lived alone in the woods in a sturdy log cabin Otis built with his father in the 1890s. Lumpy's mother was often seen in town with bruises on her face that she tried to hide with her old farmwife bonnet. She had at least two miscarriages after Lumpy was born, and speculation was that Otis was to blame. When Lumpy was seven, he came home from school and found she was gone along with her few possessions. Otis came back that evening, looked around, and said,

"Your mother left us, boy. You'll have to take care of things around the house and do the cooking. No more time for schooling."

That was all he said, and Lumpy's life of hell began. Lumpy quickly learned how to cook so that he wouldn't get a beating. He learned how to clean, sew, and split wood so that he wouldn't get a beating. He learned that he'd have to spend the night in the woods or the marsh when Otis was drinking, so he wouldn't get a beating. Lumpy's frustration and anger eventually erupted on the kids of the community.

Tommy grabbed another chair, sat beside Father Mac, and helped put the salve on Lumpy's back and shoulders. He unsuccessfully tried to hold back his tears as he applied the ointment.

Tommy had never been beaten. He'd got some well-deserved paddlings by Mrs. LaFayette at the one-room schoolhouse, but that was it. He felt he was lucky because he knew other kids that would get it pretty bad. Julio even got it a few times with the belt, but what happened to Lumpy was just plain evil.

"Ouch."

"Sorry Lumpy."

"That's ok."

"I'll be back in a minute. I need to get a wet towel and find another can of salve. You keep putting that on, Tommy."

Tommy Two Pockets
And the Posse of the Marsh

"Ok, Father."

As Lumpy lay there, he turned his head toward Tommy and said,

"Why? Why did you help me?"

"We weren't there to help you, Lumpy. We were there to punish you for Sonny and everything else you do. We just got tired of it."

"But you helped me. Why would you do that after all the crap I gave you guys?"

"I don't know. I guess when I saw what your old man was doing, I knew it wasn't right, and I guess.........I guess I had to."

"Thanks, Two Pockets. I'll never forget it."

Lumpy turned his head the other way and started crying. The crying turned into sobbing before Father Mac came back. He put his hand on his head.

"It's ok, son. Go ahead and let it out. You're safe now. I'll do what I can to make sure you never go back there. Now sit up a little bit and take this. It'll help calm you down and remove some of the pain."

He drank the apple juice laced with Mackinaw Mash.

Chapter 19 - Jimmy

He spent the last half-hour on the toilet trying to get his bowels moving. He wanted to get ahead of it so it wouldn't end up in his diaper. The embarrassment of having someone on the staff clean him up after was simply too much for his pride.

He could've just stayed in his room and not gone out, but that wasn't his nature. He had to keep moving. He had to be active. He was a hard worker - always had been. He just couldn't sit around. If there was daylight, there was work to be done. He worked construction as an ironworker. He baled hay and straw in the summer. Moved snow in the winter. Raised horses. Grew fruit trees. He taught kids in the neighborhood the importance of hard work and a job well done. When he was forced to retire at 71, because of his bad hip, he bought a five-foot circular saw and a log splitter and started a small firewood business. Everybody knew Jimmy with his slight limp, sweat-stained straw Fedora and the ever-present unlit cigar in his mouth. If they needed help with a project, they knew where to turn. He was a Jack of All Trades and Master of most. He was valuable in the community.

When his wife Dorothy died in 1983 after a short battle with cancer, his daughter and worthless son-in-law moved in with him on his small acreage so they could take care of him. Two years later, as he was losing control of his bowels, they talked him into going to the Mouillee Rest Home. He knew what they were up to from the minute they moved in. But they were in for a surprise. Once he died, the acreage and his savings would go to the Brownstown Children's Home. He checked with his lawyer Mr. Felske last week to ensure everything was still good.

Tommy Two Pockets
And the Posse of the Marsh

He was just tired now. Tired of the shit. Tired of not being able to hear anybody. Tired of not even being able to cut a straight board in the woodshop. His hip was a source of constant aggravation. His hands shook most of the time. He hated the Mouillee Rest Home. And he hated that he became a crotchety old man.

She said,

"There is another way. A peaceful way. You don't have to continue suffering."

He warmed to the idea quickly. The three pills were in a small plastic bag taped to the back of his sock drawer. He didn't know what they were, but remembered the instructions. Red, white, and Blue. About 10 minutes between each one.

"Will it hurt?"

"It shouldn't if you do it in that order."

He went to lunch and ate the same old crap they usually served. He listened to Mabel complain about her damn leaky faucet and Two Pockets never-ending wisecracks for the hundredth time. He was sick of it all. He thought to himself.

"This is what he had to look forward to day after monotonous day? Why?"

He didn't say two words through lunch, even though Two Pockets was saying something to him. He just ignored him and pretended not to hear him. He was tired of it all.

Tommy Two Pockets
And the Posse of the Marsh

When he left the lunchroom, he hadn't gone 30 ft. when Agnes stopped him.

"Mr. Cooper, I think you're having a problem."

He turned around and looked at the trail of diarrhea he was leaving behind him. His diaper wasn't tight enough and was squirting with each step. He could smell it now and just hung his head as they put plastic on a wheelchair, sat him down, and then put a garbage bag on his legs. Unfortunately, he knew the routine.

After they cleaned him up, he sat on the edge of the bed trying to collect his thoughts. He wondered why God was letting him live this long. He wondered if Dorothy was waiting for him in heaven or had found a new boyfriend. He missed her. She would know what to do.

Would they let her make peach banana torte in heaven? Was she still taking banjo lessons? Did she have a bike? Was she swimming and gardening and being pretty and....?
He hoped he wouldn't have to stand around all day singing. Never could carry a tune in a bucket. Would they even let him into heaven? He hoped so. He believed in God and Jesus and understood Christ dying for his sins, which were many.

He spent most of the afternoon napping and trying to think straight. Before he left for supper, he grabbed the plastic bag with the pills. Red, white, and blue.

"How many minutes between each one?"

He couldn't remember. "Did it matter?" He'd just take them red, white, and blue.

Tommy Two Pockets
And the Posse of the Marsh

She said.

"There is another way. A peaceful way. You don't have to continue suffering."

That sounded good to him.

Chapter 20 - The Movie

Tommy was able to enjoy Hamball Friday for a change. He figured his theory about Jimmy's reaction to the corned beef hash surprise for breakfast was correct. With a different meal, he didn't come in carrying a full load.

"Jimmy, how come you're not eating your Hamball."

"What's that Mabel?"

"Your Hamball. How come you're not eating it."

"I'm not eating it.'

"Right, why?"

"I don't need a reason why. I'm just not."

"Are you alright?"

"Of course I'm alright. Why do you have to be such a nosy Nellie, Mabel? Can't a guy not eat in peace? Geez."

Jimmy slowly got up, slammed his chair into the table, and huffed away.

"What did you do to piss him off, Mabel?"

"Up yours, Frank. I didn't do nothing. I just asked why he wasn't eating, and he got his shorts in a bunch."

"Wanna split his Hamball, Two Pockets?"

"Sure, Frank."

Tommy Two Pockets
And the Posse of the Marsh

After supper, they slowly made their way to the movie room for the "7:00 Early Show." Residents started arriving at 6:00 to get their spot. Usually, someone from a group went in and "saved" a row of seats for their friends. The saver had to be as careful as a nesting bird in a rookery. Always on alert. Always ready to go to battle to save the precious seat. After all, no one wanted to go to the "Late Show" even though there wasn't one. And with only 100 seats in the room, you didn't want to be left out, though a third of the seats were always empty. Some had their particular seat, and God have mercy on the person who sat in the wrong spot.

Several residents brought a small container with them to supper. As soon as the food arrived, they filled the container and rushed to the movie room. The staff quit trying to enforce the "No Food Allowed" sign at the door. Ruby Thompson and Ardelas Walker had an ongoing feud over the center seat 5th row back. They both figured out that this was prime real estate, and they claimed it. But the one who got it was the loser because the other one would sit one row back and talk throughout the movie, creating a shhh storm.

"Did you get it set up, Two Pockets?"

"Aye aye, Cap. Frank's the projectionist tonight, and he knows how to operate the splicing equipment. He said it was hard concentrating on which segments to add and where. Said he wanted to stay with the plot line."

"Stay with the plot line?"

"I didn't ask. He just said it's a masterpiece and the first one is 7 minutes 30 seconds in."

"Well, let's hope for the best."

127

Tommy Two Pockets
And the Posse of the Marsh

Julio, Tommy, Cap, and Gertie sat in the back row behind Mabel, sitting next to Jimmy, who was already asleep.

A few minutes before 7, everyone was ready with their small bags of popcorn that the staff handed out. Plain, no salt, no butter. They were worried about high blood pressure and cholesterol. Most residents brought a salt shaker they stole from the dining room, and some lucky residents brought spray butter. They didn't pass it around, but they gave it a squirt if you handed the sack over.

Tommy could hear George and Thelma Lou Bentley two rows ahead in their loud whisper.

"What's the movie tonight, Thelma Lou?"

"Let's see. Something about a caveman on mars."

"Will there be any skin?"

"Oh, George, stop that!"

"Just asking."

The movie starts with a shuttle from earth to mars. The large crew included Sheila, her scientist grandfather Professor Lundgren, and Brock, the wise-cracking, self-absorbed Adonis. Brock and the Professor have a falling out, and Sheila goes after Brock to tell him,

"Please forgive Grandfather. He's just set in his ways."

"He hasn't forgiven me for the problems during the last trip to Mars."

Tommy Two Pockets
And the Posse of the Marsh

"Oh, Brock. He knows it wasn't your fault. How could you know the cavemen would steal the amino acid fluid granular starch and bleach monitor?"

"Yes, but I should have known. Thirty-seven people lost their lives due to my negligence."

"Oh, Brock, you must forgive yourself."

They embraced.

"Oh, Sheila."

"Oh, Brock."

They kissed. The picture went blank for a split second, and then for the next 30 seconds, the residents were treated to a woman going for a pony ride on her partner. Her large breasts bounced up and down and slapped her in the face. All this time, the same dialogue repeats.

"Oh, Sheila."

"Oh, Brock."

"Oh, Sheila."

"Oh, Brock."

Then it cuts back to the film with Brock and Sheila making eyes at each other.

"That was a masterpiece, Tommy."

"That's what Frank said, Cap."

Tommy Two Pockets
And the Posse of the Marsh

Frank looked over at Tommy with a big smile on his face. Tommy gave him the thumbs up. The chatter in the movie room hit a fever pitch.

"Oh my!"

"Ha. Ha. Ha!"

"What was that?"

"What happened? I was sleeping?"

"I think I've seen this before."

"Was that Barbara Stanwyck? I heard she was in this movie with Fred McMurray."

"Rewind it. Play it again."

"George, where are you and Thelma Lou going?"

"Can't waste it, Two Pockets."

"Have fun!"

"What's that smell? Has Jimmy got a full load on Mabel?"

"Yeah, Tommy. That tends to happen when you die."

"What?"

"Jimmy's dead."

Tommy got up and went over to Frank behind the projector.

Tommy Two Pockets
And the Posse of the Marsh

"Better shut it down, Frank. We got a problem over here."

"What's the matter? We're just about to get to the best part."

"Jimmy's just kicked. I'll get a staff member in here."

"Oh."

The news spread through the room like wildfire. Some people crossed themselves while some mumbled a quick prayer. They slowly started to leave the room with sad faces, wondering how long before it would be their turn.

"At least he got his wish, Cap."

"What's that Mabel?"

"He wanted to die in his sleep."

As Tommy and Julio were walking back to their rooms, Julio askcd Tommy.

"Does it scare you, Two Pockets?"

"What's that?"

"Dying."

"I don't know."

"I don't think I've ever seen you scared of anything."

"I guess I've hid it pretty well."

"What have you ever been scared of?"

Tommy Two Pockets
And the Posse of the Marsh

"Otis Pies."

"Nobody would've ever known."

Chapter 21 - Rumors

Mabel stayed by Jimmy's side until the ambulance came to take him away. She watched as an EMT looked at his mouth and then got a small vial out of his medical kit. The EMT then took a tongue depressor, scraped some foam out of Jimmy's mouth, and put it in the vial. Mabel wasn't shy about much of anything.

"Why did you do that?"

"To help determine the cause of death."

"Do you always do that?"

"No. Sometimes. I only see foam in the mouth like that when a drug overdose is involved."

"Are you saying Jimmy overdosed?"

"No. I'm just taking a sample. We'll let the medical examiner make that call."

"But you just said the only time you see that is when someone overdoses."

"Well, yeah. But who knows? I'm not a doctor. I probably said too much."

Mabel slowly walked back to her room, thinking about what she had just heard. She was mumbling to herself as she went along.

"Was Jimmy on drugs or not..........Oh my God! Oh my God!"

Tommy Two Pockets
And the Posse of the Marsh

She stopped in the hallway and watched as a nurse pushed the evening pill cart through the hallway.

"Oh my God.......Tommy......I need Tommy!"

He wasn't in his room, so she went to Julio's. Not there. Then she remembered Cap inviting everyone over for a nightcap.

"Hello, Mabel. Glad you joined us. Too bad about Jimmy, but he was......"

"Just a minute Cap. Is Tommy here?"

"Yes, he's out on the deck. Can I get you some......"

"Yeah, a stiff one. Make it a double."

She went to the deck and found Tommy, Julio, Mooch, and Suds."

"Here you go Mabel."

"Thanks, Cap."

She downed the two fingers of scotch Cap poured for her and held out her glass for another. Back it went.

"Whoa, slow down Mabel. What's the matter?"

"I'll tell you Two Pockets. I think Jimmy was murdered."

"Why would you think Jimmy was murdered?"

"Because the EMT said he overdosed."

Tommy Two Pockets
And the Posse of the Marsh

"What? Why would he say that?"

"Because he had foam in his mouth."

"So?"

"The EMT said that he only sees foam in the mouth when someone overdoses."

"Ok. Maybe Jimmy got into something he shouldn't have."

"Right. Jimmy got into something he shouldn't have. And where do you think Jimmy got something he shouldn't have?"

"I don't know, maybe he went to the corner of 6th and Finkle."

"Very funny. No. I know what happened."

"Well, don't keep us in suspense."

"The pill cart. They gave him the wrong medicine, and it killed him."

Suds jumped up with his hands in the air.

"Geez Louise! I've been saying that for years! I'll tell ya; those nurses don't know what they're dishing out. Why one time, they gave me Paul Sullivan's meds by mistake, and I slept for 18 hours straight. It doesn't surprise me. No sir, it doesn't surprise me at all. Not at all."

"Slow down, Suds. Now sit down."

Tommy Two Pockets
And the Posse of the Marsh

"Aye Cap."

"This is just a theory, isn't it, Mabel?"

"Well, yeah, Cap, but what else could it be?"

"I think she's right, Cap. The same thing happened to me, except they gave me Marvella's hormone therapy drugs. I don't want to talk about what happened to me."

"Is that when you started growing those boobs, Mooch?"

"Alright, Two Pockets, that'll be enough."

"Aye Cap.......What if she's right?"

"Well, I'd rather doubt it. They have some pretty strict protocols for handing out medication."

"Yeah, but they've screwed mine up more than once."

"Well, that may be Mooch, but let's think about this. What drugs would they be passing out that could be fatal like that?"

"Strychnine? I don't know. Something like that?"

"Exactly Julio. And why would they have Strychnine or something like that on the pill cart? Who is taking strychnine for medical purposes? Nobody. No, there must be some other explanation."

"Maybe he smelled himself. I swear his farts were going to kill me."

Tommy Two Pockets
And the Posse of the Marsh

"Have some respect, Two Pockets."

"Sorry Cap. Couldn't help myself."

"Alright now. I think it best that we keep this to ourselves until we know for sure what happened. Everyone agree?"

He got "Aye, Aye's" all around and a "So right."

Of course, the rumor made it off the deck and spread throughout the home like a freight train. When the pill carts came around in the morning, there was outright defiance by some of the residents.

"I'm not taking that poison!"

"What's in those things you're giving us!"

"You're trying to kill us all!"

"You'll hear from my lawyer!"

"I want to see Ms. Haverhill!"

The staff was totally unprepared for this. Most medications were for blood pressure, diabetes control, blood thinners, and arthritis. There were no narcotics or anything else that could be considered overtly dangerous.

Roughly ⅓ of the residents refused to take their medications. At 11 a.m., two doctors from the Brownstown Medical Arts Building and a pharmacist from Bettendorf's Rexall came to try to calm everyone down. They went individually to those upset and explained the protocols they set up for the Mouillee Rest Home.

Tommy Two Pockets
And the Posse of the Marsh

"All medications are delivered once a week, and Nurse Fletcher and her staff have procedures they follow. We do unannounced monitoring quarterly, and we have never had an issue. The medications are put in the resident's medication locker in day trays. The lockers are locked, as is the room."

"Then what killed Jimmy?"

"I have no idea, but I can assure you it wasn't a medication delivered by the nursing staff."

This did little to settle the fragile nerves of the residents, who were already close to the end of their allotted time on earth and didn't want to see it prematurely extinguished. The rumors did not die down and only ramped up.

Chapter 22 - The Boot

Family members were called, lawyers were contacted, and Griz started on the White Russians early.

"Mr. Tupoc, I need to talk to you."

After another exciting lunch of boiled hot dogs on stale buns, Tommy was just leaving the cafeteria.

"Ah, Griz. Just the person I want to see."

"The name is Ms. Haverhill, and I want to see you. Come to my office."

"No."

"We need to talk, Mr. Tupoc, in private. Now let's go."

"No, Griz, I don't think I will. You got something to say, say it here."

"Alright, and quit calling me Griz."

"Fine. What do you want......... Grizzzzzzzzzz?"

"Roberta, would you call security for me? I think we're about to have a problem with Mr. Tupoc."

"You're not going to have a problem with me, Griz. Just tell me what the hell you want. I gotta get back to my room before that slop I was served for lunch hits my bowels. You don't want me doing that here, do ya, Griz?"

"I understand you showed a pornographic movie last night."

139

Tommy Two Pockets
And the Posse of the Marsh

"Me? What? You mean a skin flick? I wouldn't do such a thing, Griz, no telling where that could lead. Wouldn't want a bunch of pregnant geriatric cases walking around the rest home. I mean, what would you do with the babies? By the way, I hear they got crabs over in the east wing. You ever had the crabs, Griz?"

"Mr. Tupoc! That is quite enough!"

"It's a simple question, Griz. Yes or no?"

"You're pushing it, Two Pockets."

"I'm pushing it? What are you gonna do? Kick me out of the "Happiest Place Money Can Buy?" You come up with that dandy jingle Griz? It's about your speed."

"What a great idea."

"Well, go right ahead! Do me a favor! Boot my ass!"

A smile slowly appeared on her face, and as she walked away, she said over her shoulder,

"And you can take your little friend Juan with you."

"His name is Julio!.............BITCH!!!!"

She didn't turn around but raised the single finger flag of "Up yours."

Back in his room, he had just sat down when there was a knock on the door.

"Come on in. It ain't locked."

Tommy Two Pockets
And the Posse of the Marsh

He didn't turn around to see who it was and kept staring out the window trying to calm down. The thought of throttling the Griz was starting to win the battle in his brain as his desk chair slid into his side-view, followed by Miss Sissy. She sat down and joined him looking out at the marsh for the next few minutes. Finally, she said,

"You know why I'm here?"

"How much time did she give me to find someplace to live?"

"Two weeks."

"I'm not going into another nursing home."

"You sure? I've got a lot of contacts and can help."

"No."

"What about Julio?"

"Yeah, Julio."

"His health isn't as good as yours."

"I know."

"You need to consider that."

"Yeah. That's why I'm here in the first place. Sold my fishing boat so we could be here. So he would be taken care of, but I...........I can't do this anymore. This place is a real shithole, and you know it."

Tommy Two Pockets
And the Posse of the Marsh

"It does have its challenges."

"Why are you here, Sissy? You're better than this place."

"I uh, well, I have a history that seems to follow me around. This was the only place I could get a job when I got out of college."

"You? A history? Besides my wife Meg, you're the sweetest, most down-to-earth lady I've ever met."

She put her hand on his arm and smiled at him.

"I don't know what to say to that, but there was a time when you wouldn't think that."

"I doubt it."

"I don't...........I didn't know you were married."

"Still am as far as I know."

"As far as you know?"

"Last time I saw her and my two kids was when I went off to the war. WW2."

"Can I ask what happened?"

"I don't know. I'd get the occasional letter from her when I was out to sea, but they stopped. My letters were returned to me. When we were in Hawaii, I managed to get a call through to Julio at Black's Bay. He went to our apartment in Wyandotte, but she wasn't there. The apartment manager said she skipped out on rent and wanted Julio to pay it,

Tommy Two Pockets
And the Posse of the Marsh

which he didn't. I came back from the war six months after it ended and couldn't find her or the kids. Wasted $300 on a private dick, but he had no luck. I eventually stopped looking for her. I figured if they wanted to see me, they would know where to look. I just don't know what I did. I thought she loved me. Maybe she didn't."

"I'm sorry, Tommy."

"I still love her, Sissy. Or at least the memory of her. I've had a few girlfriends through the years, but I never got serious with any of them. I guess I'd start feeling guilty. Like I was cheating on Meg."

"You're loyal. Just like you are to Julio. Just like you are to Captain Dougherty and like you were, or are, to the *Posse of the Marsh.*"

"Yeah, I guess I am....................But, I have had this empty, hollow..... I don't know what. I feel like I missed out on life. I might have grandki.............."

Tommy put his head down and fought to hold back his emotions. Something he was never prone to do.

Sissy put her arm over his shoulder.

"Maybe I can help."

"Help? And do what? They don't want me. Why bother 'em?"

"Maybe they do want you. Maybe they wonder about you too."

Tommy Two Pockets
And the Posse of the Marsh

"No. It's too late. Please don't. Just let it sit."

"Are you sure?"

"Yeah.......yeah. Let it sit."

"Ok......We have to talk about what you are going to do. Do you know anybody that you might be able to stay with?"

"No."

"I don't know your financial situation, Tommy. How much can you afford?"

"Not much. The home takes most of what little I get in Social Security. I have a little in savings. I suspect if Julio and I pooled our resources, we could afford something. I'd sure like to find something by the water. I've always been near the water or the marsh. So has Julio. I think he'd go crazy if he couldn't see the marsh."

"Hmmm...... I might know of a place."

"Where?"

"Let me make a phone call before I tell you."

"Near the water? The Marsh?"

"Let me make a phone call."

Sissy left, and Tommy watched a pair of graceful Trumpeter Swans move along the marsh's edge. Occasionally they would dip a long neck below the surface and come up with something they would shake and swallow. He thought they were a lovely couple. Soon his eyes became heavy, and he was back in 1920 at St. Henry's Parish.

Chapter 23 - Gettin' Otis

As Lumpy was getting dressed, Dory's father ran out of the house with Father Mac behind him. A few minutes later, Doc Landrith came in along with Julio and Dory's mother.

"Where's Dory?"

"In the kitchen through that swinging door."

Doc Landrith and Mrs. Perkins went in, and Mabel came out carrying a tray with some sandwiches and apples.

"Sister Mags figured you'd be hungry."

They were. Mabel sat next to Lumpy on the couch.

"Lumpy?"

"Yeah, Mabel."

"Does he do that a lot?"

Lumpy hung his head down and slowly chewed on his sandwich.

"Lumpy? Does he?"

"Leave him alone Mabel."

"That's ok, Two Pockets. Yeah, 'bout once or twice a week. Sometimes it's not too bad, but lately, he's been getting worse. I've been thinking about running away."

"Where would you go?"

Tommy Two Pockets
And the Posse of the Marsh

"I don't know. I thought I'd try to find my ma."

"Do you know where she is?"

"No. I heard Otis yelling at her one time, saying something about what he'd do to her brother in Tawas or something like that."

"Where's that?"

"I don't know, but that's where I thought I'd go, but he'd probably figure it out and come and get me."

"Why does he do that to you?"

"I don't know. Little things. Sometimes for nothing. One day he said I was breathing his air, and he beat me."

"Is that when you choked Sonny?"

Lumpy looked up at Two Pockets.

"It's probably a good thing you and Julio were there."

"Were you going to kill Sonny?"

"I don't know. I hope not, but I don't know. I gotta tell him I'm sorry."

"Yeah, and every other kid in Black's Bay."

"I know Mabel."

They sat for a long time, then finally Lumpy said;

Tommy Two Pockets
And the Posse of the Marsh

"How?"

"How what?"

"How do I say I'm sorry?"

Sister Mags had come into the room and knelt beside Lumpy.

"Just be a friend and protector, Lumpy. They're all good kids, and I think you are too. You just have to let that side out. Talk to Father Mac. He'll know what to do."

"I ain't never been to church, Sister."

"Yes, you have. You used to come every Sunday when you were small. Your mother would bring you."

"Did Otis come?"

"No."

"Do you know why my mother left us?"

"I have a pretty good idea, but she kept to herself and never really talked to anyone I know. Was it hard for her at home?"

Lumpy put his head down again, and the tears started flowing.

"I'm sorry Lumpy. I shouldn't have said that."

"It's ok, Sister. It's just that she didn't deserve what she got, and neither did I."

"No, you didn't."

Tommy Two Pockets
And the Posse of the Marsh

"Do you have family in Tawas?"

"I don't know. I just heard that one time about an uncle in Tawas."

"So you don't know about your grandparents?"

"No."

"Maybe we can find your mother's family in Tawas. Do you know your mother's maiden name?"

"Her what?"

"Her last name before she married Otis."

"No."

"Lumpy, I guess I don't even know your mother's first name. What is it?"

"Bitch."

"What?"

Lumpy looked around and said it again.

"Bitch. Her name is bitch."

"Lumpy. No one has the name bitch."

"That's all Otis ever called her. I thought that was her name."

"Oh my." Now, Sister Mags was crying.

Tommy Two Pockets
And the Posse of the Marsh

"I failed your mother, and I failed you, Lumpy. I only knew her as Mrs. Pies. I never took the time to get to know her. I heard the rumors and didn't intervene or try to help. God forgive me."

She made the sign of the cross and then hugged Lumpy as they both let the pain in their souls come out in tears.

Doc Landrith came out of the kitchen.

"How's Dory?"

"She's good, Sister. The bullet didn't go too far in. It looks like it got her on a ricochet."

He held out the bullet that was flattened on one side.

"She'll be a little tender for a while and won't want to sit on her left side, but she'll be fine. She can walk, but probably a little slow. Mabel, would you help Mrs. Perkins get Dory home?"

"Sure Doc."

Chief Constable Mark Clark pulled up in his Model T with Constable Zmolek as they were leaving. Chief Clark, at 26, was the youngest Chief Constable Black's Bay ever had. He was elected to fill his grandfather's seat, who retired at 75 after 42 years. Chief Clark did not have the same fatherly approach to law enforcement as Grandpa Andy and, on his strong advice, kept Constable Zmolek with him at all times to temper his impulsive gung-ho spirit. Constable Zmolek's nickname was 5x5. Five-foot high by five feet wide. But he was a good man and surprisingly quick and strong for his size. He could hold his own in any tavern brawl and had a reputation for his fair temperament. The village elders tried to get him to run for Chief, but he had no interest. He was fine in his current position babysitting Chief Clark and enjoyed how he was consulted before action was taken. Chief Clark respected and admired Constable Zmolek. They made a good team balancing each other out.

They got statements from everyone and checked out Lumpy's back. Chief Clark pulled Lumpy's shirt back down and said;

"Lumpy, we gotta find your pa. If he's not out at the clearing, where do you think he'd be?"

"What are ya gonna do to him?"

"Well, we're going to arrest him. What happens from there will be up to the Magistrate."

"Do I gotta go back there?"

"I don't know that. Depends on the Magistrate. If not, we'll probably have to take you to the county Juvenile Home."

"Reform school?"

"It's not a reform school, Two Pockets."

"That's not what I hear. They gotta work on the county farms from sunup to sunset and don't get paid, and they got these dungeons, see? They sleeps three to a bunk, and they gets whipped and don't get nothing to eat but milk, mush, and beets. On Sundays, they sit in Church all day praying and telling everybody what rotten kids they are. You can't send him there, see. You can't. You just can't."

151

Tommy Two Pockets
And the Posse of the Marsh

"Now Two Pockets. I'm sure it's not all that bad."

"It is, Sister Mags. It is."

"Do I have to go there, Sister Mags?"

"Let's just see what happens, and maybe we can figure something else out."

"How old are you, boy?"

"I don't know, Constable Zmolek. I think maybe 12."

"You don't know when you were born? When's your birthday?"

He just shrugged his shoulders.

"Well, we'll have to talk about this later. Now Lumpy, the Chief asked you where we can find Otis."

"I don't know. He disappears a lot, but I don't know where he goes. He usually takes off for two days at a time, but he never tells me where he's been, and I don't ask."

"We'll find him."

Just then, Sonny came charging in the door.

"Doc Landrith, ya gotta come quick! You too Chief! It's Father Mac and Mr. Perkins, they're at the General Store! They been beaten pretty bad!"

Tommy Two Pockets
And the Posse of the Marsh

Father Mac and Gus Perkins were both laid back on sacks of flour. Both had blood running down from their head, and their faces were swelling up.

"What happened, Father?"

"Gus was going after Otis. I tried to stop him, but he wouldn't listen, so I went with him. We walked down the lane to the clearing, and Otis came out of nowhere. He had a big stick and hit Gus in the head first. Then he hit me in the stomach and doubled me over. The next thing I knew, I woke up with blood all over. I figure he hit me in the head and then hit us or kicked us in the face. Gus was out pretty good, and once I got him to wake up we staggered back. This is the first place we came to."

By now, there were at least a dozen men in the General Store.

"Let's get 'em."

"Shooting a girl and beating a priest."

"Load your guns."

"Bring a rope."

"We needs a Posse."

"Who said that?"

"I did."

"You're right, Sonny. We need a Posse."

Tommy Two Pockets
And the Posse of the Marsh

"All right, men, now listen to me. We're gonna go find Otis, but there won't be any hanging. Now I can't tell you not to bring a gun because we don't know if he'll be shooting. Anything else 5x5?"

"Yes, Chief. First of all, you boys stay here."

"Aw 5x5."

"Don't aw 5x5 me Two Pockets. I don't want no kids around. Got it!"

"Yeah, but it ain't fair."

"I see you there, you'll see how fair the bottom of my boot is. Now, don't none of you be walking around with a loaded gun. We'll tell you when to load them. I don't want nobody getting shot for being careless. And remember, we're arresting him. That's it. We're not beating him, hanging him, shooting him, or anything else. If anyone doesn't like it, stay home. Anyone breaks my rules, you'll answer to me, see?"

He cocked his hat and quickly swiped his nose for emphasis. With his hands on his hips, he looked around at the faces of all the men. They knew he was serious and not to be trifled with.

"What about tar and feather?"

He walked up to Ronny Rickle and glared at him.

"What do you think?"

"No?"

Tommy Two Pockets
And the Posse of the Marsh

"Alright now. Half of you go with me. We'll follow the bay and come up on the east side of his clearing. The rest of you go with 5x5 down the lane. When we get to the clearing, spread out and be careful. Stay behind some cover and let me or 5x5 do the talking. Now 5x5, give us a 10-minute head start before you take off. Any questions?"

"Yeah, we getting paid for this?" Ronny again.

"Any good questions? No? Let's go."

A shot rang out when both groups were near the clearing, followed by a loud cry of pain. It was the last man in 5x5's group, Archie Pavela.

"What the hell?"

"He shot himself 5x5! Archie shot himself!"

5x5 went back to where Archie was lying, his kneecap shattered. Chief Clark's group ran through the clearing toward the shot. All loaded and ready for battle.

"What happened? We heard a shot."

"Archie, what did I tell you about having a loaded gun? What a fool."

"Ahhhhhh...........Sorry......ahhhhhhhhh.......Sorry, 5x5."

"Ronny, go back and get your car and take his sorry ass out of here."

Tommy Two Pockets
And the Posse of the Marsh

"What? You want me to put him in my car, Chief? I don't want blood all over it."

"Put a damn blanket down or throw him over the hood."

"Will I get reimbursed for the gas?"

"Lord have mercy! It's a mile there and a mile back! Go get your car!"

"Go get your own! You can't push me around like that!"

"Johnny Cecil, here's my keys go get the 'T'."

"Right, Chief."

"I'm gonna remember this next Saturday night Ronny when you get all liquored up, and I haul your ass to the jail instead of your house. It's gonna cost you a hell of a....."

"There he goes!"

While they were jabber jawing, Otis ran out of the cabin and into the woods. He had a double-barrel shotgun with him, and when he saw the men crossing the clearing, he fired off one barrel. The men all scattered for cover.

"You know what's good for you; you'll leave me alone!"

"Better give yourself up, Otis. You can't get away!"

He fired the other barrel, and the men scrambled again.

Tommy Two Pockets
And the Posse of the Marsh

"5x5, you take a few men and go to the left. Ronny, you and a few men, go right, and I'll go up the middle. We'll flush him out."

"Wait a minute Chief. He's gotta gun. I ain't getting killed over this."

"Me neither!"

While they were arguing, Julio came running up.

"We got him Chief! We got him!"

"What?"

"We were waiting on the other side of the clearing. There's a worn trail. Me, Sonny, and Two Pockets was hidden over there, see? Figured that's where he'd go, see? Otis, he fires off that second shot and turns around, and me, Sonny, and Two Pockets lets him have it with our slingshots. I hit him in the nuts, Sonny got him in the nose, and Two Pockets got him in the forehead. He fell over like a sack of taters. I got another shell out of his pocket while Two Pockets grabbed the shotgun. He's holding it on him."

The men ran over to find Otis starting to come around. He was groggy as 5x5 put the cuffs on him.

Otis looked at Tommy and growled.

"I'll get you kids for this. Two Pockets, you better watch out, 'cause I'm coming for you."

"Ah, your mudda's knickers."

Tommy Two Pockets
And the Posse of the Marsh

Tommy wasn't gonna let anybody think he could be intimidated. But he was scared.

Word quickly spread throughout the small hamlet of Black's Bay that Otis had been captured. For his part, Chief Clark took no credit for his capture and made sure everyone knew it was Julio, Sonny, and Tommy Two Pockets that took him down. They became minor celebrities and enjoyed all the congratulations and way to go as they swaggered down the street. Old Man Black came out on the fish house stoop as they were passing by.

"Aren't ya 'fraid he'll come after ya when he gets out?"

Tommy, with his hat cocked to the side and, speaking out of the side of his mouth, said,

"Me and the Posse ain't 'fraid of no low down, sneaky, scoundrel like Otis Pies, see?"

Then he spat on the ground and exaggerated wiping his mouth with his sleeve.

"Whatcha mean, the Posse?"

"*Posse of the Marsh*. We'll take on the devil his self, see?"

"Pretty big talk there, Two Pockets."

"Talk we can back up."

Old Man Black came down the stairs, grabbed Tommy by the back of the shirt, and half picked him up.

Tommy Two Pockets
And the Posse of the Marsh

"Now you listen to me and listen good, Tommy Tupoc. Otis Pies isn't a man to mess with. He'd rip your head off, piss on your innards, and act like nothing happened. You got lucky this time, son. That man is dangerous, and all three of you need to be watching your backside. Now stop walking around with your chest puffed up, cause I think you just started something that Otis is gonna wanna finish. I'd lay low for a while and knock off this cocky attitude if I were you."

"You scared of Otis Pies?"

"Damn right I am, and every man in the village should be too. Look, Tommy, I just don't want you kids hurt. Now get out of here and be careful."

"He's in jail. He can't hurt us."

"You don't know what the magistrate will do when he comes next week. He might let him go."

"But he shot Dory."

"It was an accident."

"He beat up Mr. Perkins and Father Mac."

"They were trespassing."

"You really think he'd let him go?"

"Probably with a fine or something. But yes I do. So quit making all this noise and being so proud of yourself. Got it?"

"Ok. I got it, Mr. Black. I'll knock it off."

Chapter 24 - Out and About

Whenever they kept someone at the tiny two-cell jailhouse, they would have Old Martin Swenson stay through the night. He was a retired constable and far past the time when he could be of any use if trouble came up, but the village elders felt it necessary to have someone in the jail when someone was locked up. Martin could use the dollar he'd receive for being there. He carried a hearing trumpet that only marginally helped his lack of hearing.

"Can I pick what kind I get?"

"What?"

"What kinda pie do I get?"

"What pie?"

"You just said someone owes us a pie. I want cherry, but apple would be fine. Shoot, I'd even take gooseberry or rhubarb. I guess it don't matter. I'll take whatever they bring. But why do they owe us a pie?"

"I didn't say that. I said Otis Pies is in a cell. We need you to come to the jail tonight."

Martin looked at 5x5 and shook his head.

"5x5, I don't know why they owe you a pie too, but look, son, you need to lay off them sweets."

5x5 just shook his head and signaled for him to follow. When they walked in, and Martin saw Otis, the light went on.

160

Tommy Two Pockets
And the Posse of the Marsh

"You want me to stay here tonight for Otis Pies. Why didn't you say so? Better bring a piece of pie for Otis too."

As was normal, Martin would wait until the prisoner was sound asleep and then go to the other cell and curl up on the cot.

A little after one in the morning, Gus Perkins found the keys and locked Martin's cell. He quietly opened Otis' cell and approached him as he lay on his side with his back to him. As he raised the club he was carrying, Otis suddenly turned and kicked Gus in the groin.

Martin never woke during the commotion, and when Chief Clark came in the next morning, he found Martin sitting on his bunk with his arms folded and tears coming down his face. Gus was lying on the floor with his skull caved in in the other cell. Otis was gone.

The county Sheriff was notified, and by ten that morning, the area was swarming with Sheriff's deputies and two men from the fledgling Michigan State Constabulary, forerunners of the Michigan State Police. It was determined that Otis Pies was a dangerous man and needed to be apprehended quickly. The village elders came together and announced a reward of $100 for information leading to the arrest of the miscreant Otis Pies.

$100 was a lot of money in Black's Bay at that time. Many men in the community fancied themselves as instant bounty hunters and when it came time to raise a "posse," not too many were interested. They wanted the reward all to themselves. As a result, the woods and marshes surrounding Blacks Bay were suddenly filled with armed men looking to make a quick buck.

161

Tommy Two Pockets
And the Posse of the Marsh

At 5:30 the next morning, just as dawn broke, Dusty Peterson made his way to the outhouse. He froze in his tracks when he heard a shotgun being racked.

"Stop right there, or I'll shoot! Put your hands in the air! Gotcha, Otis Pies! You're coming with me!"

"I've known for years that you're a damn fool, Leo Peterson. I'm your brother, for God's sake. Put that away."

"Well, hell. In this light, you look like Otis from the rear."

"You're still a fool."

"Don't call me that!"

"Fool."

They both had to visit Doc Landrith.

Clyde and Mitch Feral spent the night in the marsh, paddling around in a canoe with a lantern looking for footprints or boat marks on one of the numerous tiny islands. They finally found an old canoe on a bank and snuck up on Pete Navarre, sleeping by a small campfire. Clyde kicked him in the side.

"Get up there, Otis. We all are taking your ass in."

All 6'5" and 300 pounds of Pete got up as Clyde and Mitch realized their mistake and were putting their pistols away. That was a bigger mistake, and both ended up visiting Doc Landrith.

Several incidents were reported to Chief Clark, who reported to the village elders that their reward scheme was backfiring

Tommy Two Pockets
And the Posse of the Marsh

and should stop it. They wouldn't hear of it with all the families scared out of their wits that a killer was on the loose in the community. None of them wanted to be the one that didn't do all they could to bring in Otis Pies, notorious varmint and killer. Not with elections coming up in the fall.

"How much is $100 split five ways?"

"Why just five ways? What about Dory, Two Pockets?"

"Mabel's right. Should be six ways."

"Now wait a minute, she ain't here. Why should she get a share?"

"Because I said so, Lips LaRue!"

"Who made you the boss, Mabel?"

"You're asking for it, Lips."

"Ok. Stop it. Dory is part of the Posse. She can't help it if she gets shot. She's still getting her share."

"I think it should only be split four ways anyway. We can't have no girls with us when we bring in Otis."

Mabel was on Lips like a fox on a rabbit. He didn't stand a chance. Tommy and Julio pulled her off as Sonny sat laughing.

"Stop it Mabel. You say something like that again, Lips, they'll be pulling me off ya, see?"

"Geez. Ok. Forget it."

Tommy Two Pockets
And the Posse of the Marsh

"So how much is it split six ways, Julio?"

"$16.66. I say we each take $16 and give Lumpy $4."

"Why give Lumpy anything?"

"Cause he ain't got nothing at all, Lips. Mmmmmm.......What would it be if we split it by seven, Julio?"

"That would be........$14.28 with 4 cents left over."

"But...."

"Shut your face, Lips. Do I run the *Posse of the Marsh* or not?"

"Yeah, but how come we don't get to vote?"

"Because you can't vote unless it's on the ballot and the election ain't til this fall."

"So, Two Pockets, are you saying we should let Lumpy be in the *Posse of the Marsh*?"

"That's right, Sonny."

"Even after he choked me and all the other crap he's done?"

"That's right."

"I'd still like to hang him."

"You ain't hanging nobody, Lips."

"Yeah, but it ain't fair."

Tommy Two Pockets
And the Posse of the Marsh

"Maybe, but I'll tell ya. I'd rather have him on our side than against us, wouldn't you?"

"Yeah, but still."

Mabel stood up and said.

"I know Lumpy's done a lot of things that hurt us all at one time or tother, but I feel sorry for him. He ain't got no family or nothing, and well...... It just seems like the right thing to do. And Two Pockets is right. I think he'd be a better friend than an enemy. And if you're worried that he'll take too much share of the reward money, he can have mine."

Tommy stood up next to her.

"He can have mine too. He ain't got nothing."

Then Julio stood up and said,

"So right. He can have mine too."

Lips and Sonny looked at each other. Finally, Sonny stood up and joined them. Lips shook his head.

"Look at you guys. Couple of days ago, you wanted to teach him a lesson. Now you want to give him $100."

"We didn't know what he was going through a couple of days ago. We just wanted to hate him without knowing the kinda' of shit he was going through. I think we should've known."

"You should be a nun, Sister Mabel."

Tommy Two Pockets
And the Posse of the Marsh

Tommy let Mabel beat on him a few minutes before pulling her off.

"Lips, why do you keep doing that? Maybe I should just let her have at ya and be done with it."

"There's one thing we're forgetting Two Pockets."

"What's that Julio?"

"We gotta catch Otis."

"Yeah."

Tommy sat and scratched his head.

"What are you gonna do, great leader?"

"Stuff it, Lips. We need to talk to Lumpy."

"Where is he?"

"He stayed at the Kramers last night."

"Go get him, Julio."

"I'll go with him."

"Ok, Mabel, we'll wait here."

They were already in the Kramer's shed, so it didn't take them long to return with Lumpy.

"How was it last night?"

Tommy Two Pockets
And the Posse of the Marsh

"Nicest place I ever slept. I guess it was their daughter's room. Mrs. Kramer said she ran away last year. Sixteen years old, they said. Came home from Mass, and most of her things was gone. She didn't want to talk about it. I was gonna go sleep in the woods, but Sister Mags had already talked to Mrs. Kramer, and they wouldn't let me. Last night, Mr. Kramer's boat came in, and I heard them talking downstairs. I heard her tell him that I could stay as long as needed, and he thought that was a good idea. I think so too. Boy, did I have a swell breakfast! Something she called french toast and Canadian bacon."

"Can I move in too?"

"Me too!"

If the rest of the posse had breakfast, they were lucky to get a bowl of Farina or leftover fish from the night before, if it kept.

Tommy asked him, "Did you hear your pa broke out of jail and killed Dory's father?"

"Yeah. Mr. Kramer says I should lay low for a while 'cause some people will want to take it out on me."

"Stick with us, you'll be ok. We gotta find him. Will you help us?"

"Sure. No telling what he'll do now."

"Any idea where he may have gone?"

"Maybe. He takes off once in a while, and I followed him out in the marsh one time. He'd packed up the good canoe with

167

supplies. I saw that and wondered where he was going with all that stuff. So I took the old leaky canoe out and went after him. He went back around Crow Island and then disappeared. I couldn't find the canoe or where he put in or anything. But I'm guessing he's around there somewhere."

Crow Island was an overgrown sandbar hidden deep in the marsh. If you were just looking at it from the water, you would never know there was land behind the dense, heavy brush. It was a little over 10 acres, with the widest part at about 150 yards.

"Have you told anyone else this?"

"No."

"I've never heard of Crow Island. How do you know about it?"

"That's just what Pa called it. There's a catfish hole near there that we'd run trotlines on. Crow Island was the landmark."

"What's on Crow Island?"

"Nothing I know of. Just a bunch of brush and undergrowth."

"Look, Lumpy. We plan on catching your Pa and collecting the $100 reward. You wanna help us?"

"Help catch my Pa?"

"Yeah, that's what I'm asking."

"I don't think that's a good idea."

Tommy Two Pockets
And the Posse of the Marsh

"I know he can be mean and ornery and stuff, but I think we can do it if we're smart about it."

"I just don't think you know how mean he can be."

"How 'bout if we find him and then tell Chief Clark? We could still get the reward."

"I'd do that."

"Ok, we'll get Old Man Black's rowboat and see if we can figure out where he went."

"Won't work. There are some narrow cuts that only a canoe can get through. We could take our old leaky birchbark canoe, but I don't think it could handle more than three of us."

"Ok, I'll go and........Mabel, you wanna go?"

"What's wrong with me, Two Pockets? How come you pick a girl and not me?"

"Cause she don't asks stupid questions, Lips."

"You want her to go 'cause she's your girlfriend!"

"Sic him Mabel."

An hour later, Lumpy, Mabel, and Tommy set off in the canoe and turned around after 100 yards. The canoe had a major leak along the keel in the bow. It was probably there for quite a while, but undetectable with only one person in the back of the canoe. With two more holding the bow down, the leak became very apparent and unbailable.

Tommy Two Pockets
And the Posse of the Marsh

"I can fix it, but we won't be able to go till tomorrow morning."

"Ok Lumpy. Let me help."

"Both of you can help by standing guard and making sure Otis doesn't show up."

Chapter 25 - The Threat

It was another long day at Black's Fish House for Gladys. Three mixed loads came in that morning, consisting of mostly rough fish. She was assigned to one of the worst jobs of gutting the rough fish before going into the grinder. Her assignments were an unstated punishment for rebuffing the advances of Mr. Mowry, the shop foreman who would come by and pinch and slap her behind at every opportunity. She fantasized about accidentally turning around with the filet knife, gutting him, and throwing him into the grinder.

She knew she would get help in the process from more of his victims. She also decided that she had enough and planned to talk to Mr. Black about Mowry even though she may lose her job. At 4:30 that afternoon, as the last whistle blew, she made her way up to Mr. Black's office and knocked on his door. She opened it, and Mowry was standing behind him by the desk.

"Yes, Mrs. Tupoc, what is it?"

"Can I speak to you alone, Mr. Black?"

"Of course, Mr. Mowry and I just finished up. Will you excuse us, Mr. Mowry?"

As Mowry walked past Gladys, he reached behind her and squeezed her bottom. She turned and slapped him hard on the face.

"What's this? Gladys, why did you do that?"

Tommy Two Pockets
And the Posse of the Marsh

"He grabbed my ass, and I'm tired of it! He does this all the time and not just to me, and we're all sick of it. The man is a pervert."

"Now wait a minute, I did no such thing, you lying whore!"

"Mowry, you wait outside and close the door. Have a seat Mrs. Tupoc. Now tell me what's going on."

Gladys watched the door as she sat down, holding back the tears that wanted to come pouring out.

"He thinks we're his personal harem, Mr. Black. Some of the girls give in to him for better jobs, but most of us don't want that creep near us. He's always trying to play grab-ass with us or touching our breasts. It's hard enough work without that crap."

Old Man Black sat back, sighed, and rubbed his face.

"I'll be honest with you, Mrs. Tupoc, I've seen him do it a few times, and I regret saying I have turned a blind eye. I'm sorry. I'll put a stop to it............ Ok. You go home now, and here, take this down to the packaging table and pick out a couple of fish for your supper tonight. Give it to Evelyn. She'll take care of you."

"What about Mowry?"

"My guess is he is standing outside with his ear to the door listening. Don't worry about it, Gladys. I said I'll take care of it, and I will."

"I believe you. Thank you, Mr. Black."

Tommy Two Pockets
And the Posse of the Marsh

Mowry was outside the office and gave her the stink eye when she went by. Old Man Black shouted:

"Come back in Mowry, and close the door!!!"

That evening after fixing the whitefish and cornbread, she went to her normal perch on the back stoop and stared into the trees with her small goblet of Mackinaw Mash. It was not doing its job of taking the edge off the anxiety and melancholy that tightly gripped her mind.

She was sick of Mowry and the stinking work at Black's. She was essentially sick of being on her own and constantly scraping to get by. She was sick of being a terrible mother but didn't know how to change that. She was sick of Black's Bay, her clothes, the rundown house, the bitches she worked with, being lonely, and having nothing to hope for. She was sick of her miserable life. She thought about the 20 gauge sitting behind her on the stoop and the peace it would give her.

"Why not?" She said to herself.

"Who would miss me? Who would care?"

Her courage grew with every glass of the mash. Well into her 5th round, she heard something moving in the dark woods. A small sound. A twig or branch breaking. A quiet intake of air. A grunt.

She grabbed the 20 gauge,

"Is that you, Mowry?! I've got a gun, and I'll use it!"

Tommy heard her and came out on the stoop.

Tommy Two Pockets
And the Posse of the Marsh

"What is it, Ma?"

"Somebody's out there in the woods, moving east. It might be Mowry. I had some trouble with him today."

"Otis. It might be Otis."

"Turn off the lights in the house, Tommy."

Their eyes were adjusting to the dark, and Tommy started to make out a man standing 40 yards away by a tree.

"There, Ma. Someone is standing there. See him?"

"Yeah. Get outta' here. I've gotta gun!"

The shadowy figure moved, and they could hear him heading east again.

Then they heard in the distance, "Don't go to sleep, Tommy Two Pockets. I'll slit your throat."

Gladys fired two rounds in that direction.

"You stay away from my boy, Otis Pies!"

She let two more rounds go. Then they heard voices heading their way. A group of men had been sitting on the dock by the fish house.

"What are you shooting at, Mrs. Tupoc?"

"Otis Pies! He said he was gonna slit my boy's throat! You gotta get him! He's heading that way towards his cabin! You gotta get him!"

Tommy Two Pockets
And the Posse of the Marsh

One of the men ran to the church and rang the bell. Soon there was a large gathering at the fish house.

"Alright, everyone, settle down."

"We gonna hang him this time Chief?"

"Next person that says anything about hanging, I'll throw 'em in jail."

"Yeah, but I got shot because of him, Chief."

"You got shot 'cause you're a damn fool, Archie. We told you not to walk around with a loaded gun. Now, I need four men to go with me out to Pies clearing. The rest of you stay here. 5x5 set up a guarded perimeter around the Tupoc's. You stay with them 5x5. He comes back, I want you there."

"Ok Chief."

As they were getting ready to leave for Pies clearing, Red Tompkins came running up.

"I've been robbed, Chief! Somebody's been in the General Store."

"Probably Otis."

"Near as I can tell, he took a bunch of staples and been in the gun case. Took a couple of handguns, a LaFever Nitro Special 12 gauge, and a Remington 30-30."

Tommy Two Pockets
And the Posse of the Marsh

"Ok, boys, if he's that armed, we're calling in the county and wait til morning. We ain't getting ourselves shot up. He got what he came for, so I don't expect he'll be back."

"He said he was gonna slit my boy's throat, Chief. You can't just let him run around out there."

"Gladys, you and the boy come over to our place tonight and bunk. Marsha'll be happy to see ya. Got an extra bedroom, and I got a cot for Tommy."

"I don't want to put you out none 5x5."

"Won't be no problem, Gladys. Now get your things together, and let's head over there."

"That's real good 5x5. Now the rest of you. I know there is a reward for Otis, but now that we know he is heavily armed, I don't want any of you going out there and getting yourself killed. We all know Otis is a rough character and dangerous without a weapon, so steer clear of him and go home."

They mingled for a few more minutes, then slowly made their way home. Word quickly spread around the tiny hamlet, and the already edgy townspeople didn't get much sleep.

Chapter 26 - Crow Island

Tommy met Mabel and Lumpy at the newly patched-up canoe just before sunrise.

"Mr. Kramer wasn't going to let me out of the house, but he didn't have much choice cause I had to use the outhouse. I think he sat in the kitchen all night, keeping an eye out. He came out on the back stoop and watched me. He was sleeping when I was done with my business, so I took off. Hate to do that to 'em. They been pretty nice."

"Yeah, but we gotta find your Pa."

"I know. So let's go."

With Lumpy in the back, Tommy upfront, and Mabel in the middle, they took off in the old birch bark canoe Lumpy had fixed the day before. It was watertight and seemed to silently float across the water.

Lumpy and Tommy quickly got into a rhythm using a ten-count switch and could feel the cadence of each other's strong pull on the paddle. Mabel let one hand touch the water and watched the minute wake it created.

The marsh was waking up around them. A small flock of geese greeted them as they made a sharp turn through the marsh. The sudden sound of the annoyed honking geese seemed to wake up the other members of the marsh family - a beaver, several muskrats, ducks, and turtles resting on half-submerged logs. Fish rising for the early banquet of hatching Mayflies on the water. Simultaneously Tommy and Lumpy quit paddling as they approached a beast rarely seen though well known to those who ventured into the marsh. A

Tommy Two Pockets
And the Posse of the Marsh

Bobcat was standing on a log, concentrating on something in the water. As quietly as he could, Lumpy put the flat of the paddle blade 90 degrees into the water to slow the canoe down and stop them.

They were within 20 yards of the Bobcat before it noticed them. It tilted its head side to side as if he was curious about what was interfering with his potential morning meal. He then turned his attention back to the water and pulled a bluegill out of the water and into his mouth with one swift stroke of his paw. He held it there and looked back at the canoe as if to say, "Can you do that?" Then he turned toward shore and plunged quietly into the marsh with one mighty leap.

It was going to be a cloudy overcast day, and they could feel the moisture in the air. They knew rain was coming.

"How long before we get to Crow Island, Lumpy?"

"Probably another ½ hour or so, Mabel. I think when we get near to it, we oughta not talk until we figure out where he might be."

"Ok."

They pushed their way through a narrow channel to a large marsh pond. On the other side was Crow Island. Tommy whispered,

"What do you think, Lumpy? Is he around here?"

"I don't know, but let's paddle around the Island and see if we can see anywhere he might have put onto shore. If you see something, don't talk. Just use hand signals. Let me do the paddling."

They headed to the right of the Island, and all they could see was the heavy sumac, red cedar, wild berry bushes, reeds, and cattails that lined the shore. They couldn't see past the heavy brush onto the Island.

Mabel whispered to Lumpy.

"You sure about this?"

"No. Just keep looking."

After 20 minutes, when they were just about the full circle around the island, Mabel signaled with her hands to back up. There she pointed out a place where reeds were broken, and it looked like a narrow opening into and under the brush. Tommy pointed to the sumac branches, and it appeared that someone had cut them 2 ft above the waterline.

Lumpy brought the canoe to line up with the narrow opening and motioned for Tommy and Mabel to get low in the canoe. He pushed into the opening and got into the bottom of the canoe, reaching up to grab the branches and push them forward. Tommy was doing the same from the front, and after a few minutes, Tommy grabbed a branch and stopped them. He pointed ahead to the back of a canoe on its side. Otis's canoe.

They slowly moved forward to get a better look, and to their amazement, they saw three small flat top buildings in a clearing. One looked like an outhouse, another a storage shed, and the largest a small cabin. Smoke was coming out of the chimney, and as they were watching, they could see a faint light come on in one of the tiny windows. It started to rain, and Tommy signaled that they should go up and take a look. Mabel signaled that they should leave. Lumpy just sat there.

Tommy started to get out of the boat when the outhouse door opened, and there about 50 yards away, stood the Kramer girl looking at them. She put her hand up to her face and started to cry.

Chapter 27 - Kidnapped

"You sure you don't mind staying home this week sweetie?"

"No ma go ahead I'll finish dinner and everything will be ready when you and pa bring back Father Mac and Sister Mags."

"Well alright, but I don't feel right about this. Maybe you should go with your pa and I'll stay home."

"Don't be silly. What's the matter? Don't you think I know how to make mashed potatoes and biscuits?"

"Well alright, just keep an eye on that roast."

"I will Ma. Now go on, Pa's waiting outside for you."

He'd been watching her for the past month patiently waiting for the right opportunity. He was an expert at staying in the shadows, a skill he learned in Cuba.

He knew exactly how many Spaniards he dispatched with his knife. 53. He would just disappear in the evenings while everyone was trying to find something to eat or prepare a place to sleep out of the rain and mud. Everyone got used to the strange look on his face and his blood-stained clothes. No one bothered him, no one questioned him. Not even the noncoms and the officers. He saw no point in charging the enemy in a full-frontal attack so he didn't, and no one wanted to confront him about it. But he was in his element at night in the shadows. He would occasionally don a Spanish uniform, go to their camps, find something to eat, and leave another unsuspecting victim. This was an opportunity to take as many lives as he wanted with no repercussions. How could he be so lucky? He didn't want it to stop, but after being there only three months, the war ended.

Otis stood looking at the Kramer house between a boat in dry dock and an old shed. He watched as Mr. and Mrs. Kramer walked to St. Henry's. Most of the people in Black's Bay would be at mass, but where was she? He walked to the house, stood by the coal chute and peaked through the window. She was making mashed potatoes. Good. She could cook. He went around to the back door, which he didn't expect to be locked. No one locked their houses in Black's Bay. She was singing to herself and banging pots and pans around, covering any sound he made.

He slipped up behind her and put the burlap bag over her head and held her tight with one arm as he looped a rope over her head tying her securely in the bag. He then put a towel around her head to muffle her screaming. He took a second rope and tied her legs together. He laid her on the floor and ran upstairs looking for her room. He quickly grabbed as many things as he could to put in his seabag. For effect, he grabbed a couple of pictures and her diary which was lying on her nightstand.

He went back downstairs and hoisted her up over one shoulder with the seabag on his other. He walked across the path to the bay, roughly put her in the bottom of his canoe, and set off for Crow Island.

She had no idea who had her or where she was going, but she was terrified. When she tried to struggle she would get a hard kick, so she stopped. Between the lack of air and her rapidly beating heart, she finally passed out. When she woke

Tommy Two Pockets
And the Posse of the Marsh

his face was right over hers as he had positioned himself to take her. Her arms were tied to the frame of the bed. She screamed and he slapped her.

He grabbed her face and turned it to the left.

"See that girl standing there? Scream again or resist me and she will die. It's up to you if she lives or dies."

"Listen to him. He'll kill me. Please just do what he says."

Her eyes felt like they were coming out of her head.

"Please don't."

He slapped her again.

"Don't talk! Now do your duty!................ Save the girl."

She couldn't stop crying, but she did not resist. She couldn't hold back a scream as he entered her, resulting in another slap. The other girl shrank to the floor holding herself and mumbling incomprehensible words.

To Nadine the minute it took for Otis to reach his peak, seemed a lifetime. He got off her and left the cabin as the other girl helped her get off the bed so she could change the bloody bedding.

"What's your name?"

"Huh?"

"Sh......Whisper......What's your name?"

Tommy Two Pockets
And the Posse of the Marsh

"Where are we?"

"Sh... Keep your voice down. He might not like us talking.......I don't know where we are."

"You don't know?"

"Please whisper.........On an island somewhere in the marsh."

"Who are you?"

"Wilda. Who are you?"

"Nadine. Why are you here?"

"He kidnapped me last fall."

"Where are you from?"

"Erie, by the Ohio border. Where are you from?"

"Black's Bay."

"Never heard of it.........I think he's gonna kill me now that he's got a new girl. There was another girl when I got here and then she was gone. I think he killed her."

"I have to get out of here."

"You can't. If you do, he'll kill your family."

"Otis wouldn't kill my family."

"That's his name? How do you know his name?"

Tommy Two Pockets
And the Posse of the Marsh

"Cause he's the wood cutter at Black's Bay. Him and his son."

"He has a son?"

"Lumpy. Lumpy is his son."

"How old is he?"

"I don't know."

That evening, Wilda dropped a plate of caramel rolls. It did not go well for her.

Chapter 28 - Left Behind

Tommy signaled for her to keep quiet and to come to them. She looked to the cabin, signaled that Otis was inside, and shook her head. Tommy turned to Mabel and Lumpy.

"I'm going to get her. If Otis comes out, go back to Black's Bay and get help."

"No Two Pockets......"

But it was too late. He went left along with the brush and around the shed, coming up behind Nadine Kramer out of sight of the small windows in the cabin. She was shaking.

"I can't go; he'll kill my family and me."

"No, he won't. We won't let him."

"He's done it before. I saw him kill Wilda."

"Wilda. Who's Wilda?"

"Another girl he kept out here. Just go. Leave before he sees you."

The rain came down harder. Tommy could barely make out the canoe with Mabel and Lumpy.

"It doesn't matter. You have to come with us. He killed another man in town."

"No, you don't understand. Go and get help. Tell my parents where I am. Please just leave."

186

Tommy Two Pockets
And the Posse of the Marsh

Tommy grabbed her by the arm and started pulling her toward the canoe. She struggled, and then the door to the cabin opened slightly.

"Girl, where are you?!" Otis yelled.

Nadine pushed Tommy away and motioned for him to go. She walked toward the front of the cabin.

"Coming."

"Where you been?"

"Outhouse."

"Well, get your ass in here, fix me some breakfast, and hurry up about it."

Tommy could see Otis as he came out of the house and looked toward the canoe landing. He stood, cupping his hands over his eyes to block the rain as if he could see something. Tommy ducked behind the shed and watched, expecting Otis to head to the landing; but instead, he shook his head and went into the cabin.

Tommy slowly made his way back to the landing and looked in the tunnel. They were gone.

Chapter 29 - Marsh Journey

When Mabel saw the cabin door start to open, she ducked down and motioned for Lumpy to back out into the brush tunnel. Halfway through, they hung up in some bush. Mabel peeked over the top edge of the canoe and could see Otis off in the distance looking their way. She motioned for Lumpy to be quiet and pointed to Otis. Finally, he went into the cabin, and Lumpy and Mabel managed to get the canoe loose and continued through the tunnel. Once on the other side, Mabel said;

"We have to go Black's Bay and get help."

"We can't leave Two Pockets there. Pa'll kill 'em."

"He can take care of himself. We have to go back now!"

"Ok."

They'd gone about 200 yards when they sprung a leak on the starboard side of the canoe.

"We must have done that when we hung up."

Mabel panicked as water started rushing in faster than she could bail.

"What do we do Lumpy?"

"Come back here. We'll put all the weight in the back and lift the front of the canoe. Maybe we can get the hole above the water line."

Tommy Two Pockets
And the Posse of the Marsh

She went all the way back and got behind Lumpy, but it did no good. The hole got bigger, and within minutes the canoe was submerged. They were in 3 feet of water as they got out of the canoe and quickly realized they couldn't stand in the muck on the bottom as it oozed around their feet and sucked them in like quicksand. Lumpy managed to pull his feet up and float on his back. Mabel was stuck and going down. Within seconds her mouth was below the waterline. She started to scream in the water. Lumpy sucked in a deep breath, put a brawny arm around her, and spun from face up to face down in the water. Mabel came up and crawled on Lumpy's back, pushing him down toward the muck. With three powerful strokes of his arms and legs, he pushed himself away from her and came up for air. Mabel was still struggling and starting to lose the battle again.

"On your back Mabel. Float. Put your head back and look at the sky. That's right. Just look at the sky. Feel the rain on your face."

He did the same thing, maneuvered himself by her head, and said calmly,

"It's alright, Mabel. Just relax. I won't let anything happen to you. Trust me."

"Ok. I'm scared."

"Me too, but we have to relax and take deep breaths. Just breathe. I've got you."

"Ok."

Lumpy looked around and saw a small fallen tree near the water's edge by the marsh reeds.

189

Tommy Two Pockets
And the Posse of the Marsh

"Mabel, I'll pull us over to that small tree. We can hang on to it while we figure out what we're going to do. Just stay on your back and let me do the work, ok?"

"Ok. Just don't let me drown."

"I won't."

Lumpy flipped over on his stomach, grabbed the back of Mabel's collar, and started to swim toward the fallen tree 50 yards away on the edge of the marsh pond.

"Grab this, Mabel, and pull yourself up."

There was just enough room for Mabel's upper body on the exposed fallen trunk. Lumpy tested the bottom and found it was the same muck they just got out of, so he grabbed a branch and floated as best he could.

"How will we get to Black's Bay, Lumpy?"

"We have to find something to float on or swim."

"We can't swim. It's too far."

"It took us well over an hour to get out here in the canoe, so I'm guessing 4 to 5 miles. We have to find something to float on. Either way, we have to keep moving. Look. You're already shaking. Do you know how to swim?"

"I can dog paddle or breaststroke."

"Ok. We'll have to swim until we find something we can float on."

Tommy Two Pockets
And the Posse of the Marsh

They got back in the water, careful not to touch the bottom. Mabel moved slowly, and Lumpy had to hold back so she could keep up. After fifteen minutes, Mabel had to stop.

"I can't.....I can't!"

"On your back, float on your back."

Lumpy pulled her along for another 15 minutes until he had to stop. They both floated on their backs for a while and, once rested, started again.

"I'm freezing Lumpy. I can't keep going."

"We have to Mabel. Look, the rain stopped, and the clouds are breaking up. The sun's going to come out."

"I can't."

"Float on your back again."

Lumpy once again drug her along. He could see the narrow passageway that led into the pond and headed in that direction. He knew the water was shallower there and hoped he would be able to walk on it. The bottom was not any better and only 2 ft deep. Not enough to swim in and too soft to walk on.

"Listen Mabel. We'll have to float on our sides, grab the reeds, and pull ourselves along."

"I don't think I can."

"You have to."

Tommy Two Pockets
And the Posse of the Marsh

"Leave me here and go back for help."

"No, I can't do that. You have to come with me."

"I can't Lumpy. I can't go any farther."

"MABEL, YOU'RE COMING! Now get on your side and pull yourself along! Do it!"

Crying, she slowly turned on her side, grabbed the cattail's base, and pulled herself forward. Lumpy did the same on the other side of the narrow passage, occasionally reaching back and pulling Mabel ahead. He was getting to the point of exhaustion himself and didn't know how much farther he could go. After several minutes, Mabel was no longer pulling herself along, relying on Lumpy to move her forward. As they came to the end of the 200-yard-long passage, Lumpy saw a beaver lodge in the middle of the next marsh pond. As they approached the lodge, he tested the bottom again, and there wasn't one. The water was well over his head. At the lodge, he told Mabel,

"Grab this and keep your head up."

He crawled up on the side of the mound, then reached down and pulled Mabel beside him. She was shaking, and her lips and skin were blue. He knew he needed to warm her up. He took off his shirt, wrung it out the best he could, and wrapped her in it. The sun finally peaked out from behind a cloud. They both could feel its warmth. Lumpy did his best to rearrange the debris on the lodge enough for a comfortable place for Mabel to lie back on. She quickly fell asleep as the sun's rays warmed her up and dried her off. Lumpy laid back as well and was soon asleep.

Tommy Two Pockets
And the Posse of the Marsh

He woke up when he felt Mabel touching the scars on his back.

"I'm sorry, Lumpy."

"Why? You didn't do anything."

"I just am. Nobody should be treated like that."

"If I ever have kids, I'll never hurt them. I don't want them to be afraid of me."

"Yeah. I bet you'll be a good father."

"I hope so."

They lay there a few more minutes, feeling the sun.

"Look, Mabel. We're going to have to get back in the water. The sun is starting to get low, and we have a long way to go. We can't stay here in the dark. We need to go as far as we can."

"Ok."

"I'm gonna free up some of these small logs and see if we can float on them."

Lumpy started tugging at the lodge and managed to free up three four-foot by eight-inch diameter pieces of cedar. He took off his rope belt and was able to strap the logs together in the middle. The branches on each end meshed together enough to secure it from coming apart. He put it in the water and had Mabel crawl on top of it. There was only enough room for her, so he went back into the water and pushed them both along. He felt strong once again after their rest and started moving at a decent speed. He knew he had to keep Mabel dry so she would not give in to the cold when night came. Within an hour, the sun was gone, with only a sliver of moon to take its place.

"Mabel, are you awake?"

"Yes."

"Can you see anything?"

"A little."

"Do you see the opening for the next creek out of here?"

She squinted and finally said,

"I think it's over there."

"Keep pointing to it, and let me know if I'm not going in the right direction."

Another 10 minutes, and they were at the mile-long creek entrance that would take them to the edge of Black's Bay. Once there, they still had to cross the bay. Lumpy figured at least another 2 hours. He could hear Mabel shivering again and knew he had to get there as fast as possible.

A light misty rain started again. Not heavy, but enough to soak Mabel. Lumpy tested the bottom and found that it was firmer but deeper. He couldn't get a footing while keeping his head above the waterline, so he continued to swim. A quarter of a mile in, there was a loud splash as something jumped

Tommy Two Pockets
And the Posse of the Marsh

out of the marsh and bounced off Mabel's back as she lay on the small makeshift raft. They both screamed, and Mabel fell into the water. Lumpy realized the bobcat they saw earlier used the raft to jump across the narrow creek. Lumpy managed to get Mabel back on the raft.

"Lumpy......"

"What?"

"Lumpy...... I'm hurt."

"What?"

"My back. I'm hurt."

Lumpy reached up and felt her back. Her shirt had been ripped, and he could feel the warmth of her blood as it oozed out. The bobcat claws had dug into her back when it jumped across. He could tell she was losing blood fast. He had to do something to slow it down. He reached down and scooped up some of the bottom muck and put it on her back. He did this three more times until he was able to pack a thick solid layer of mud over the cuts. She didn't complain.

"That feels good, Lumpy. It feels warm."

He had seen Otis do this once when he sliced his leg open with a machete. It stopped the bleeding and helped with the healing.

He kept pushing her slowly along but was worried he wouldn't get her back fast enough.

"Mabel......Mabel.......Mabel, wake up!"

Tommy Two Pockets
And the Posse of the Marsh

He shook her shoulders, then turned her face to his. He could tell she was still breathing. He was scared. He finally decided he had to go on without her if she was going to stand a chance of surviving the night. He talked to her one more time.

"Mabel….. I have to leave you here…….Mabel….Do you hear me?"

She was unresponsive. He pushed her into the marsh reeds to make sure she wouldn't float away.

His arms were aching. He couldn't feel his legs, but he knew they were working. He was going as fast as he could, trying to ignore the pain throughout his body. After 40 minutes, he came out of the creek and could see the lights of Black's Fish House more than ½ mile across the bay.

"What was that?"

"What?"

"Quiet. Listen."

"What? I don't hear nothing."

"SHHH……"

"There. Hear that?"

"Yeah………somebody's yelling….sounds like help."

"Where?"

Tommy Two Pockets
And the Posse of the Marsh

"Out in the bay."
Old Man Black and his night cleaner Jacob had just come out on the stoop when Jacob first heard Lumpy yelling across the bay.

"Jacob get the row boat. I'll get a lantern."

Within minutes they were heading in the direction of the voice. Jacob was rowing, and Old Man Black sat in the bow with the lantern.

"Hello........ Who's there?....... Hello......... Who's there? Stop rowing.....quiet."

They listened and faintly heard "Help."

"Over there Jacob. It's coming from that cut in the marsh."

Jacob steadily rowed toward the cut while Old Man Black held up the lantern. When they were just about to the cut, they saw a hand.

"My God boy, what are you doing out here?"

Lumpy grabbed the side of the boat and pointed back up the creek.

"Mabel."

"What's that?"

"Mabel."

"Mabel? Is Mabel up there?"

Tommy Two Pockets
And the Posse of the Marsh

"Yeah."

"Get in here."

Jacob and Old Man Black reached down and pulled Lumpy into the rowboat. He was shaking, didn't have the energy to sit up, and sank to the bottom of the boat.

"Is Two Pockets with you? Everybody's been looking for you kids all evening."

"Mabel. Go get Mabel."

With that, he pointed up the creek and collapsed.

Chapter 30 - Trapped

After Otis went into the cabin, Tommy made his way back to the edge of the undergrowth, keeping an eye out for Otis. He was 50 yards to the east of the landing and found that he could not be seen if he crawled. He made it to the tunnel and found Lumpy and Mabel were gone. He looked at Otis's canoe on its side and figured if he was really fast, he could turn it over, get it to the tunnel, and be gone before Otis saw him.

He crawled over to the canoe, and just as he stood up to turn it over, the cabin door opened. Tommy went to the ground and crawled back to the brush tunnel. Otis walked to the landing in rain gear carrying a fishing pole and a small tackle box. Tommy kept backing into the tunnel and realized Otis was heading his way. He was afraid to make too much noise running in the water or swimming, so he crawled up into the sumac branches. Otis quickly had the canoe in the water and laid on the bottom on his back. He reached up and started pulling himself through the brush tunnel.

Tommy took a deep breath as he lay above the tunnel in the branches of the Sumac. He watched as the canoe moved under him. Then saw Otis's face pointing in his direction. Otis's eyes were closed. As Otis moved along, grabbing branches, pieces of bark and debris fell on his face, so he knew to keep his eyes shut and feel around for the next branch. Tommy waited for the canoe to exit the tunnel. Then he climbed back down to the water. He made his way out of the tunnel and ran up to the cabin.

"Where did he go?"

"He went fishing so we could eat. He won't be gone long."

Tommy Two Pockets
And the Posse of the Marsh

Nadine made Tommy stay outside so he wouldn't make a mess in the house or leave any indication that he'd been there. Tommy was soaked and needed to warm up, but he understood.

"I think Lumpy and Mabel probably went back to Black's Bay for help."

"You can't stay here."

"Can I hide in that shed?"

"No. When he gets back, that's where he'll clean the fish."

"Where can I go?"

"I don't know. Just hide!"

"I'm hungry. Do you have anything to eat?"

"Stay here."

She went inside and came back with two biscuits.

"Here. If I took any more, he'd know."

"This is enough."

"You better go now."

"Alright. It shouldn't take them long to bring back some help."

"Just keep hidden in the meantime."

Tommy Two Pockets
And the Posse of the Marsh

Tommy decided to see if there was anything he could use in the shed before Otis got back. He found a small folded sail, 20 feet of thin rope, and an old knife with a broken handle. He took them and went to the west side of the island. He found a space big enough to sit deep in the sumac. He had a clear view of the cabin, landing, and surroundings.

He cut a piece of the canvas sail and fashioned a small low canopy in the Sumac branches to protect him from the rain. He cut another piece to sit on and wrapped himself in the rest of the sail. He figured Lumpy must have gone back for the Chief, so he prepared to wait for them. He ate the two biscuits and then dozed off, waking a few hours later when he heard Otis turn the canoe on its side.

He watched Otis take his catch to the shed. He pulled out a small table and then stood with his hands on his hips. Eventually, he scratched his head and walked back to the cabin. Tommy said to himself,

"The knife. He's looking for the knife."

Otis got to the cabin and stopped before opening the door. He looked at the ground and then got down on one knee.

"Get out here!"

"What?"

"I said get out here!"

He was still kneeling when she came out, and he grabbed her bare foot and moved it next to something on the ground.

"Who was here?"

Tommy Two Pockets
And the Posse of the Marsh

"What?"

"Who was here? This ain't your footprint."

"I don't know." She started crying.

He stood up and slapped her hard enough to knock her down. He reached down, grabbed her long hair, and slapped her again.

"Who's here?"

"Me, you son of a bitch!"

Tommy had come out of the Sumac, took careful aim with Otis's .28 caliber pistol, and fired. At 40 yards, he had no chance of hitting him.

"Two Pockets!............... YOU'RE DEAD NOW!"

Otis ran into the cabin, and Tommy went back into the Sumac. When Otis came out, he carried the 12 gauge double-barrel shotgun. Tommy expected Otis to come after him, but instead, he went to the landing, grabbed the canoe, and dragged it to the shed. He put it inside, closed the doors, and locked it with a big padlock. There was no way for Tommy to leave Crow Island.

After Otis stored the canoe, he walked back to the cabin and went up to Nadine, still sitting on the ground, grabbed her by the hair, and drug her inside.

Tommy made his way back into the Sumac to retrieve the pieces of sail, using the rope to bundle them together. He knew he couldn't stay there, so he ran way behind the back of the cabin and headed to the other end of Crow Island.

He went deep into the Sumac, Red Cedar, and thick thorny berry bushes, the water up to his knees. He thought he was probably safe there and figured Otis was too big to crawl through the snarled branches and brush as he did. Then he started to wonder about Nadine. Otis was mad, hit her hard, and was probably still giving it to her. He didn't know how long it would take for help to arrive. He had to do something. But what?

The rain stopped, and the sun broke through the clouds. He heard the cabin door slam in the distance and knew Otis would be looking for him. He checked the pistol. He had two shots left and figured he would only use them if Otis was close up. He had to distract Otis, get back to the shed, get the canoe, get Nadine, and get off the Island. But how? Would Nadine even come with him? He finally figured the best thing was to stay hidden and hope help came soon.

He was cold and knew he had to get out of the water. He took a piece of the sail and cut holes around the outer edge. Then he ran the rope through the holes and tied it up in the branches, making a mini hammock big enough for him to curl up in. As the shadows fell, so did the temperature. He covered himself up with the rest of the sail and listened as the marsh transitioned into night.

It calmed him, and he started to doze off when in the distance, he heard,

"I'll find you Two Pockets! I'm gonna slit your throat! Then I'm gonna find your Momma and slit her throat! I'll find you! I'll find you! You hear me Two Pockets? I'm going to slit you and your Momma's throat from ear to ear! You better believe it, Two Pockets!"

He didn't feel safe anymore.

He peeked out from under the sail and saw the light from a lantern through the dense undergrowth. It was moving in his direction.

"I know where you are, Two Pockets! I'm coming! I'll be slitting your throat soon!"

Then he heard Otis hacking at the Sumac and brush with a machete. He was breaking through the undergrowth and heading toward him. He could see the lantern only 30 yards away. He slipped out of his tiny hammock and back into the water as quietly as he could. He took two steps and fell.

"There you are! Won't be long now!"

Tommy started weaving his way through the Sumac, trying to avoid the thorns of the berry bushes that already had him bleeding from head to toe. He didn't care how loud he was now. He just knew he had to get away and fast. He could barely see anything and had to feel his way along. He hoped he was going in a straight line away from Otis and not turning back to him. As long as Otis kept hacking and talking, he knew he was going away from him. Then Tommy realized that Otis wouldn't know where he was heading if he quit making noise. He stopped, pulled out the pistol, and waited. Then Otis stopped. Tommy could see Otis raise the lantern and move it back and forth, looking into the dense growth. Then the lantern went out.

Tommy Two Pockets
And the Posse of the Marsh

"Ok, Tommy. Want to play a game? Let's see who can find who. How quiet can you be? I can be very quiet, and I can still find you. You think I can't get through because it's so thick in here? Is that what you think? Let's find out. Here I come to slit your throat!"

"Yeah? Come on, you Son of a Bitch, I ain't afraid of you!"

As soon as Tommy said it, he regretted it. He was afraid of him, and between the cold water he was standing in and listening to Otis, he was shaking like a leaf. He decided to waste one of his bullets and fired one in Otis's direction, thinking it might make him think twice about coming ahead. It was answered by a blast from a shotgun that stole the sound of the marsh. Above and around Tommy, debris fell from the branches hit by the shot. Then Tommy had an idea. He wasn't hit, but he wanted to make Otis think he was.

"Ooooh! Ooooh! You got me, you bastard! Ooooh!"

Then he made a big splash in the water like he'd fallen over.

"Don't die on me, Two Pockets! I gotta slit your throat."

He waited until he heard Otis moving in his direction. He'd lit the lantern again and was hacking at the Sumac. Tommy gave it one more groan for good measure. Then as quietly as he could flanked Otis in an attempt to get behind him. He knew that as long as Otis was working his way through the brush, it would hide any noise he was making. Tommy held his breath as he came within 10 feet of Otis hacking his way through. He waited and followed the opening Otis had hacked back to the clearing. As he moved away from Otis, he could still hear him hacking away. When Tommy made it to the clearing, he started running to the cabin. He stopped and could still hear Otis in the distance.

Chapter 31 - The Posse of the Marsh

"What's the scoop Doc?"

"I think we'll know in the morning, Chief. She's barely got a heartbeat going. She lost a lot of blood and has hypothermia. I had to put 40 stitches in her back. She makes it through, she'll never wear a backless evening gown."

"That's too bad...........What about Lumpy?"

"Hypothermia. He's a tough kid. Smart too. I don't know if Mabel would have made it if he hadn't put that mud pack on her back. He should be ok. I gave him some medicinal liquid. He's sleeping pretty hard."

"Did he say what happened or anything about Two Pockets?"

"No. He was pretty well out of it."

"Can I talk to him?"

"Well, the medicinal liquid was Mackinaw Mash."

"Oh."

"Why don't you come back at sunup. Father Mac is going to sit by his side tonight. I'll tell him if Lumpy wakes up to get you."

"Ok. I'll bunk at the jail so I'll be close by. Thanks, Doc."

"Night, Chief."

"Doc."

Tommy Two Pockets
And the Posse of the Marsh

"Father Mac......Father Mac.....Wake up, Father Mac."

"Humpf........Lumpy.......Lumpy how do you feel?"

"Mabel."

"She's at her house."

"Is she ok?"

"Hard to say. Doc says she had to have 40 stitches in her back and had hypothermia. What happened?"

"Bobcat...... We have to go back.....Two Pockets.....We have to get Two Pockets."

Lumpy started to get up.

"Slow down, Lumpy, it's.....four in the morning."

"We have to go now."

"Where?"

"Crow Island."

"Where?"

"Crow Island."

"Never heard of it. Where is it?"

"We found Otis. Two Pockets is there. So is the Kramer girl."

Tommy Two Pockets
And the Posse of the Marsh

"The Kramer girl?! You stay right here! I'm going to get Chief Clark!"

"Lumpy. Come on Lumpy, wake up."

"Huh, mmmmm............. Chief."

"Lumpy. Come on. Father Mac says you found Otis, and the Kramer girl is there?"

"Yes and Two Pockets. We had to leave him behind."

"Where are they?"

"Crow Island."

"Crow Island? I've never heard of it. Where is it?"

"Four or five miles out in the marsh."

"Can you show us where it is?"

"Yeah."

"Father Mac, go ring the bell at the church. We need to get some men together to go out there. After you do that, can you go to the Kramer house and let them know about their girl? I'm going to the general store to call the Sheriff's office. Tell anybody you see to meet at the fish house."

Chief Clark and Father Mac left the house, and Lumpy slowly got up and put on his still-damp clothes. He was hungry, and his body ached, but he was determined to find out about Mabel and get Two Pockets.

Tommy Two Pockets
And the Posse of the Marsh

He made his way to Mabel's house and knocked on the door. Her mother answered and immediately grabbed Lumpy and hugged him.

"Mabel told me what you did, Lumpy. You're a hero!"

"Yeah? How is she?"

"Come on. I'll let her tell you."

They walked into a small bedroom where she was lying on her stomach facing the wall.

"Mabel....Mabel, Lumpy is here."

She turned up on her side and put her arms out for Lumpy. He slowly went forward, and she grabbed him around the neck and whispered in his ear,

"You saved my life Lumpy. You're my champion. I'll never forget it."

Then she kissed him on the cheek. He slowly stood up and put his hand to where she kissed him. He was stunned. Affection from anyone, including his mother, was something he'd never experienced in his 12 years on earth. He suddenly saw Mabel as an angel. He would do anything for her. He determined at that moment that he would always be her protector.

"Lumpy.....Lumpy!"

"Huh?"

"Lumpy, are they going back for Two Pockets?"

Tommy Two Pockets
And the Posse of the Marsh

"I don't know. They're rounding up a bunch of men. I think so. I had to come here first to make sure you're ok."

"I will be. I'm just tired."

"I need to find another canoe so I can go back."

"Lips has one. Are you going to wait for the Chief and the men before you go?"

"Yeah, I think so, but I don't want to wait too long."

"Better get going then."

"Ok."

Lumpy just stood there looking dreamy eyed at Mabel.

"Lumpy, you need to go. Why are you looking at me like that?"

"What?"

"Why are you looking at me like that?"

"Like what?"

"Like you just swallowed a toad."

"Nobody's ever kissed me before."

With that, a tear came down Lumpy's cheek. He wiped it off, gave her a big smile, and left. Mabel was staring at the door, not knowing what to think or feel.

Tommy Two Pockets
And the Posse of the Marsh

It was still dark when Lumpy walked up the steps to Lip's house as his father was coming out, shotgun in hand.

"Boy? What's this about you finding Otis and the Kramer girl?"

"Two Pockets is out there too. We had to leave him."

"What's the name of this place they're at?"

"Crow Island."

"Where's that?"

"In the Marsh about 4 or 5 miles somewhere to the south."

"Well, I'm going to meet up with Chief Clark. I hear tell we're gonna wait for the Sheriff to show up. Lord knows how long that'll take. Wouldn't surprise me if the road was washed out with all that rain last night. What are you doing here?"

"Looking for Lips."

"Who?"

"Ah, I don't know his name. Everybody calls him Lips."

"Oh, you must mean Leonard. Just sitting down for breakfast. The Mrs. is making flapjacks. You et yet?"

"No."

Mr. LaRue went back up the stairs, opened the door, and yelled.

Tommy Two Pockets
And the Posse of the Marsh

"Phoebe, fix this boy some breakfast. He's the one that saved the Navarre girl from that bobcat and found Otis and the Kramer girl. I'm headin' off to the fish house."

After a quick breakfast, Lumpy and Lips went outside.

"We gotta take your canoe and go back."

"The old man will have my hide."

"Tell him I made you do it."

"I don't know."

"Then I'm takin' it."

Just then, Julio came running up.

"Lumpy, the Chief is looking for you. Told me to tell you to get your ass back to the fish house right now."

Lumpy got an exasperated look on his face, kicked a stone, blew out some air, and said,

"Alright."

"Lumpy, there you are. Can you show us where Crow Island is on this map?"

The map only showed the general location of the marsh in relation to the land and Lake Erie.

"Well, I don't know. I ain't never seen a map before, Chief."

"How far did you say it was from here?"

Tommy Two Pockets
And the Posse of the Marsh

"I'm not sure. I guess four, maybe five miles."

"Which direction?"

"I'm not sure about that either. Just somewhere south. I just know what creeks through the marsh to follow. It ain't easy."

"Where's Johnny Cecil? Johnny, get over here."

"Whada' ya need, Chief?"

"Johnny, you probably know these marshes better 'n anybody. You know about this place he's talking about."

"What did you say the name of the island is, boy?"

"Crow Island."

"Ain't never heard of it. What's it look like?"

"Looks like it's all overgrown with sumac and red cedar. Doesn't look like there's any cleared land from the water, but there is. There's a cabin and a couple of outbuildings on it."

"Chief, I don't know what the boy's talking about. Lots of overgrown islands, but I ain't never seen anything like that out there. Don't know of any with a cabin on it."

"Well, you're going to have to show us where it is, Lumpy."

"Ok, let's go."

"Hang on. We ain't going till the Sheriff shows up, and with the road out, I don't know how long that will take."

Tommy Two Pockets
And the Posse of the Marsh

"But, Two Pockets is out there, and so's that Kramer girl."

"And so's a rifle and a shotgun."

The men kept talking, and Lumpy slipped away, followed by Sonny, Julio, and Lips.

"We can't wait Lumpy."

"I know Julio. I ain't waitin'. Lips, I'm taking that canoe, and don't try to stop me."

"I won't 'cause I'm going with you."

"Me too."

"Ok Julio. What about you Sonny?"

"Yep."

Lumpy inspected the canoe before they got in. It was a well-worn but well-maintained cedar canoe built for carrying cargo. He didn't know that the bulging sides were called sponsons, but he knew it made the canoe very stable and relatively slow. It was a 19-footer and had a keel made of a hard maple strip to help with steering such a long canoe. Lips told him this was his grandfather's canoe and designed in the French-Canadian style. He said when the family gets together, they still tell the old stories of the Voyageurs and the great adventures they had. Lips thought this was going to be a great adventure to tell his grandchildren someday.

When they left Black's Bay, the sky lightened up in the east. Lumpy was in the stern, Lips in the bow, and Julio and Sonny in the middle. All four were experienced paddlers and got into a smooth rhythm following the cadence that Lips set. Keeping the paddles away from the canoe side, they were silent except for the "pum..........swish, pum..........swish, pum..........swish" as the paddles entered and left the water at the same time. At the beginning of each stroke, they reached forward as far as possible, put their shoulders into it, and used the frame braces to push back with their feet. Lumpy could feel the steady, balanced pull resulting in a much faster pace than expected. The steadiness of the canoe allowed him to spend most of his time paddling instead of steering. Even with the danger that lay ahead, Lumpy smiled.

Lumpy soon realized that the canoe sat higher in the water than the birchbark canoes and would not fit in the brush tunnel at Crow Island. They would have to make a different plan.

When they went around the east end of the island, he remembered it tapered off into a point. The underbrush and trees were not as thick there. He didn't know if they could get through from that side, but it was worth trying. Besides, he thought it was probably too dangerous to go up the brush tunnel with Otis prowling around.

As they came to the pond where Lumpy had lost the old birchbark canoe, he told everyone to stay very quiet and let him do the paddling. He went left toward the east end of the Island and, after 15 minutes, found a place where they could drive the canoe up into the sumac and wild berry bushes.

Chapter 32 - Rescue

Tommy opened the cabin door, and in the dimly lit cabin, he found Nadine lying on a bed. Her face was bloodied, her left eye swollen shut. Her lips were bulging out of proportion.

"Geez....... Nadine, we have to get out of here."

"Na, I ca go. I ca."

"Come on, get up!"

"I ca. He bo ma ba."

"What?"

"He bo ma ba."

"Bo ma ba? Bo ma ba? He broke your back?"

She nodded yes.

Tears came to Tommy's eyes. He'd seen a lot of bad things, but never anything like this. His pity quickly turned to anger, and the anger turned to rage.

"Ge hep."

"Get help. Yes, I'll get help. Where's the key to the shed?"

She pointed over his head by the door.

"Go!"

Tommy Two Pockets
And the Posse of the Marsh

Still crying, he gave her one more look. Grabbed the key and ran out the door.

He went to the shed and could still hear Otis hacking away in the distance. He opened the doors and dragged the canoe back to the small landing. It took all his strength, but he finally managed to get it in the water. He lined it up with the tunnel and gave it a hard push.

It was starting to turn to daylight as Otis made his way back to the cabin. Before opening the door, he noticed something was not right at the shed. He walked toward it and saw the doors were open. He went inside and found the canoe gone.

"Damn him."

He walked out of the shed, and Tommy was standing there pointing the small pistol at him.

"Put down the shotgun Otis."

"YOU CAN KISS MY ASS!"

With that, Otis started to raise the shotgun, and Tommy fired. Though Tommy was only 10 feet away and pointing at his chest, he jerked the pistol as he fired and struck Otis in the left shoulder. Otis held onto the shotgun with his right hand as he went down on one knee in pain. Otis glared at Tommy and, through gritted teeth, said,

"You bastard!"

He started to raise the shotgun with his right arm as Tommy threw the pistol hitting him in the chin. Otis let out a loud bone-chilling scream that Tommy could feel through his

Tommy Two Pockets
And the Posse of the Marsh

whole body. Otis raised the shotgun again as Tommy ran around the corner of the shed. He was heading back to the island's east end when the ground exploded around him as Otis fired the first round in the double-barrel shotgun. Another 25 yards, and the second round went off. Tommy could feel the wind of the shot over his head. He turned around and looked as Otis struggled to reload with one arm. Tommy made it to the overgrown Sumac and fought his way into it as another shot rang out. This time he felt a pain in his right leg and knew he'd been hit, but he didn't stop. As the thick Sumac started to thin out, he heard;

"Two Pockets!"

In front of him were Sonny, Lips, and Julio. Behind them was the big cedar canoe.

"We heard the shots. Where's Otis?

"Coming behind me. It'll take him a few minutes to get through the brush. Let's get out of here!"

Lips looked around.

"Where's Lumpy?"

"Lumpy's here?"

"Yeah, but where did he go?"

"Can't wait. Get in the canoe. Otis is getting closer!"

As they turned to go to the canoe, there was another blast of the shotgun and Julio went down.

Tommy Two Pockets
And the Posse of the Marsh

"NOOOO!!!" Tommy yelled.

He turned around, and Otis was reloading the shotgun with one arm.

"I think instead of slitting your throat, Two Pockets, I'll just blow your head off."

As he started to shut the reloaded shotgun, Lumpy came flying at him from the side and slammed into him with all his weight knocking him to the ground. The shotgun flew, and Tommy ran over to help as Lumpy flailed away on Otis. Otis managed to grab Lumpy by the throat with one hand and started squeezing. Tommy kicked Otis in the head and then kicked him in the wounded shoulder. As Sonny picked up the shotgun, Lumpy went to work on Otis' face until it was a bloody pulp. All the time, Lumpy was crying and screaming.

"I'M A GOOD KID. YOU SON OF A BITCH! YOU DIDN'T HAVE TO BEAT ME! YOU DIDN'T HAVE TO BEAT ME! YOU DIDN'T HAVE TO.........!"

Finally, Tommy realized Otis was unconscious and put his arms around Lumpy. He held Lumpy, who kept bawling,

"You didn't have to.......You didn't have to......."

While Sonny held the gun on Otis, Lips helped Julio get back to the canoe.

"Far as I can tell, Two Pockets, Julio got hit by two or three pellets. One in the butt and one or two above his hip."

"Ok, Lips. You alright, Julio?"

Tommy Two Pockets
And the Posse of the Marsh

"So right, but it hurts like hell. Hard to move my leg."

Tommy grabbed the rope on the small anchor in the canoe and, between him and Sonny, managed to secure Otis in case he woke up. Lumpy sat off to the side, whimpering. Tommy looked around.

"Alright, listen up. He beat the Kramer girl pretty bad. She thinks Otis broke her back. Lumpy, if we load Otis into this canoe, do you think you and Sonny can take him and Julio back?"

"Yeah. Let me take the shotgun."

"Ok. Lips, you and me are gonna try to get the Kramer girl in Otis's canoe and get her back to Black's Bay. Lumpy, paddle over by the tunnel and wait there so we can follow you out of here."

"Ok."

They roughly managed to get the unconscious Otis into the bottom of the Cedar canoe, then Tommy and Lips headed off to the cabin. Tommy told Nadine what had happened, and she cried with joy. Though she was in an immense amount of pain, she managed to get to her feet and made it to the landing with the help of the two boys. Tommy went into the tunnel and retrieved the canoe. They made a soft bed with three heavy blankets on the bottom of the canoe.

As they paddled along, Otis came to, sat up, and struggled with his ropes. Lumpy pointed the gun at him.

"What are you gonna do, boy? Shoot your own Pa? Well, go ahead. Hmmmmff!"

Tommy Two Pockets
And the Posse of the Marsh

Otis looked at the other canoe with Tommy in the back.

"You think this is the end of it, Two Pockets? Not by a long shot. I'm gonna hurt you in ways you can't imagine. I'm gonna hurt you, Two Pockets. Just remember that. Don't ever forget it, Two Pockets. You are really gonna hurt."

Tommy looked at Otis and decided there was only one thing to do.

"Shoot him."

"What?"

"Shoot him Lumpy. Just shoot him."

Lumpy looked at Tommy and then at Otis.

"Yeah, ok."

Lumpy checked the two shells in the chamber and slowly raised the shotgun.

"Julio, move to the front of the canoe with Sonny and lean to the right."

"By God, you're going to do it, aren't you, boy?"

"Yes. I think I am."

Lumpy leaned to his right and pointed the gun at an angle to Otis so he wouldn't hit the boys in the front. As he put his finger on the trigger, a canoe shot out of the small creek leading into the pond.

Tommy Two Pockets
And the Posse of the Marsh

"We found them! We found them!"

Lumpy pointed the gun in the air as two more canoes came out of the creek carrying Chief Clark, 5x5, and several other men, including Nadine's father, Mr. Kramer.

When they pulled up beside Tommy's canoe, Mr. Kramer reached down and touched Nadine, who grabbed his arm and said,

"Hi, Daddy,"

Mr. Kramer moaned,

"My baby...........my baby. What did he do to you?"

Just then, Julio yelled out;

"He's loose! He's loo...."

Otis managed to get out of the rope, turned the canoe over, grabbed 5x5's canoe, and flipped that over. In the confusion, nobody noticed that Otis was swimming for the marsh bank.

"There he goes over there."

As he found firm ground and headed into the marsh, Mr. Kramer stood up in his canoe and fired his Colt Revolver hitting Otis in the right arm. Then Chief Clark knocked him down with his 12-gauge. They righted the two canoes and started to get back in them. Chief Clark, Johnny Cecil, and Ronnie Rickles went after Otis in another canoe. He wasn't there. They followed the blood trail until it ran out and decided to come back with the sheriffs tracking dogs in the morning. Chief Clark was sure he couldn't have gone too far.

After about a ½ an hour, they made their way back to the canoe and noticed a commotion where the other canoes were. As they pulled up to them, they saw Mr. Kramer and Lumpy in the water holding the edge of a canoe with one hand and pulling on something in the water.

"What's going on? What are you doing?"

"It's 5x5, Chief. He got stuck in the bottom, and it pulled him under. Don't jump in. It'll pull you under too. It's like quick sand down there."

He jumped in anyway and held on to the side of his canoe as they maneuvered over to help. They managed to get a rope under his arms and, with great effort, pulled him out and into a canoe.

When Chief Clark got back into the canoe, he yelled.

"DAMN YOU, OTIS PIES!!!!"

Chapter 33 - Goodbye Party

Although the birthday party only lasted a little more than an hour, it was already a long day for her. She found it hard to concentrate on the conversations going on around or directed to her. Too much noise. Too much chatter. And her entire body ached. She never thought your hair could hurt, but it did. Arthritis had complete control of her body, and when they put that squirming little brat on her lap for a photo, she just about screamed. As the party went on, she began to lose her politeness.

"Grandma, you look great."

"I look like shit."

"Mom, you want some lemonade?"

"I want a shot of Scotch."

"Look, Ma. Sheila lost 60 lbs."

"Where?"

"Isn't this a great party, Ma?"

"It'll be great when it's over!"

She loved them all but wouldn't miss them, and she knew they wouldn't miss her. Maybe Arthur would a little. He was a good boy. But for the rest of them, she was just an inconvenience. She understood that and knew they would be happier with her gone.

Tommy Two Pockets
And the Posse of the Marsh

But Arthur came through. A bottle of Glenfiddich. She held onto it and buried it beside her leg in the wheelchair. Couldn't let the staff get their hands on this. She waved Mabel over and whispered in her ear.

"I need you and Julio and Tommy Two Pockets to come to my room tonight at 9 o'clock."

"I'll make sure they're there."

"Good. We're going to open this bottle." She said with a twinkle in her eye.

Back in her room, they propped her up in her bed so she could eat her supper on the movable tray. She just looked at the rubber meat and overcooked green beans.

"No more of that garbage." She thought.

At 8:00, she managed to get her legs over the side of the bed then with her walker she made it to the bathroom to relieve her bowels. She found getting back into bed daunting, so she sat down in one of her easy chairs. She wanted to start on the Glenfiddich but knew she would have to wait. Her arthritic hands wouldn't let her open it. Finally, at 9:00, there was a knock on her door.

"Come in."

"Hello, birthday girl."

"Happy birthday."

"Tommy, can you open this?"

Tommy Two Pockets
And the Posse of the Marsh

"Sure."

"There's some glasses over on the counter by the sink—ice in the freezer. I'll take mine neat and make it a double. And put a straw in it. I'm having a little trouble bending my arm."

"Sure, anything else?"

"Just pull up some chairs and gather around."

Julio hobbled over to the other easy chair and slowly sat down while Mabel grabbed two folding chairs by the window. Tommy brought the drinks over and sat next to Mabel.

"Mabel, see that little cup with the pills on my nightstand? Could you get the red one out and put it in my mouth?"

"Sure, what is it?"

"Just some medication I have to take."

Nadine swallowed it, followed by another long pull on the straw. She looked at each one and, with a sigh, said.

"I've tried not to discuss it for 67 years, but there is something I need to talk about tonight. Oscar knew I'd been kidnapped, but I never told him the details. And he never asked. I don't think he would have married me if he knew everything."

"Oh sure, he would have Nadine. Oscar was one of the sweetest men I've ever known."

"He was, Mabel, but I don't know. I always thought Oscar was God's way of paying me back for what I went through.

Tommy Two Pockets
And the Posse of the Marsh

But, there is something else I want to clear up. It's about Arthur."

"You don't have to go there, Nadine."

"Well.....I'm gonna go there, Mabel. I need to. Arthur was six years old when he came to live with Oscar and me."

"Nadine, I think everyone knows."

There was a long pause while Nadine took another sip of the Scotch.

"That is what I loved about the people of Black's Bay. In all those years, no one ever asked me if Arthur was Otis's son, but that's what they think, isn't it?"

"Yeah, there have been rumors. Lumpy figured out he was his half-brother, and he treated him like that."

"Lumpy treated Arthur real good. I knew why and I just let him believe that."

"What do you mean, you let him believe that?"

"He wasn't Otis's son."

"What? He even has a resemblance to Lumpy."

"I know. I don't know why. His father doesn't look like that."

"What are you saying, Nadine? Was there someone else?"

"You know I was in Escanaba with my Aunt Connie and her husband, Uncle Jack. I had gotten my bandages off my back about two weeks earlier, and the doctor said to put some hot compresses on it once a day. I went to the backyard and laid down on a blanket with a compress on, and then I heard,

"Hello there. I'm Benny. You must be Nadine."

And there he was. The neighbor's son, Benny. Home from college. Handsome, polite. We started talking. Well, mostly, I listened. He was a big distraction from the torment I was still going through. Lunch time came, and I asked if he wanted to go in and get a sandwich. And.......well."

"Oh, my....."

"It was just that one time, but it must have been the right time to give me a gem like Arthur."

She looked at the pills in the cup.

"Mabel, please put that white pill in my mouth."

"Sure. Just what are these pills."

"Oh, they're to help me relax so I can go to sleep."

Mabel put it in Nadine's mouth, who took another pull on the straw.

"So this Benny is Arthur's father?"

"Yes. I never told him or his parents. Aunt Connie, bless her heart, she figured it out. I mean, I got pregnant almost five months after the rescue. So she came up with a plan. Once I started to show, I was to stay in the house. Well, Aunt Connie convinced me that I was in no mental shape to be

229

raising a child, so.............After Arthur was born, I went back to Black's Bay. Aunt Connie and Uncle Jack told everyone they were adopting a baby. They could never have kids. Well, it seemed like the best thing to do."

"I remember when Arthur came to live with you and Oscar. What happened to your Aunt Connie?"

"She was diagnosed with Leukemia."

"Did Oscar know Arthur was your child?"

"Yes, I told him right after he proposed to me. I told him about Arthur and Benny. I didn't want him to think he was Otis's. But it didn't seem to matter to Oscar. He was a good man."

"Does Arthur know?"

"Yes. I told him when he was 20. I thought he needed to know. Maybe he would want to meet his real father. After he thought about it, he said Oscar was his father. Why does he need two?"

By now, Nadine was starting to slur her words.

"Better take it easy on that Scotch, Nadine."

"Ha, ha. Well, who cares, Two Possitts."

"See?"

Nadine's face then turned sad, and as she looked around at her three friends, she started to cry. Mabel moved close and put her hand on her lap.

Tommy Two Pockets
And the Posse of the Marsh

"What's the matter, sweetheart?"

"Other than that business with Otis, I think I've lived a pretty good life. Do you think I have?"

"Nadine, you've lived a good respectable life from where I sit. You raised a great family, and look at all you did for the community of Black's Bay. I mean, they even named that new playground after you. "Nadine's Happy Place." You were mayor of Black's Bay for how many years, 36?"

"Thirty-eight."

"Ok, 38. Look at what you accomplished with the paved streets, sewers, street lights, the town beautification project, etc. You were exactly what Black's Bay needed, Nadine."

"Thanks Tommy............I love Black's Bay. Even with what happened to me there. It was the people. Father Mac and Sister Mags and Old Man Black. You know he covered all my medical bills."

"Old Man Black did? Doesn't surprise me. He was the best."

"Yeah, Whoeyo (Julio), the besh."

"Wow."

"And Laee. Suntines see Otis in him. Physquey I me. Ba, he had the swee soul. He mussa ga da fra his modda. He lu oo Maple. How lawn you mary?" (And Lumpy. Sometimes see Otis in him. Physically I mean. But, he had a sweet soul. He must've got that from his mother. He loved you, Mabel. How long you married?)

231

Tommy Two Pockets
And the Posse of the Marsh

All three of them had to lean in to hear and understand Nadine by now.

"Fifty-one wonderful years."

"Gray. fi-one." (Great 51)

"I miss him. You know, he never laid a hand on the kids or me in all that time. We never had a serious argument about anything."

"Can you blame him? Who'd wanna argue with you?"

"Stuff it Two Pockets."

"I'm kidding Mabel. Lumpy was great. I miss him too. I'll never forget when the *Posse of the Marsh* dealt with him and how things turned around. That day changed everything."

"He never wanted to talk about his life with Otis. He tried to act like it never happened, but sometimes I'd wake up in the middle of the night, and he was gone. I'd go downstairs and find him crying. Try as he might. He couldn't totally escape it."

"Netha coo I.......I........I..." (Neither could I)

"Nadine, I think those pills and Scotch are getting to you. Can we help get you in the bed before you fall asleep?"

"Mmmm.....Yeth, yeth."

They slowly got her into the bed and pulled the blankets snuggly up to her neck.

Tommy Two Pockets
And the Posse of the Marsh

"Nadine, I hope you had a happy birthday. We're going to go now and let you sleep."

"No.....way." (No.....wait.)

"What."

She motioned for Tommy to come close to her and whispered in his ear. He slowly stood up, looked at the cup, and then at Mabel and Julio.

"I don't know, Nadine."

"Plea...Tom......"

He looked at his friends, the cup, and back to Nadine.

"Are you sure?"

"Yeth."

"What is it Tommy?"

"I'll tell you in a little bit."

He got the blue pill and put it in her mouth. Then he put the glass of scotch up to her lips. After taking a long pull on the straw, she smiled at Tommy as a tear ran down her cheek.

"Good bye Nadine."

"Tommy, why are you saying goodbye?.............. What's in those pills?"

"She said they were to take away the pain forever, Julio."

Tommy Two Pockets
And the Posse of the Marsh

"What? What are you saying?"

"It's ok, Mabel. She wants to go."

"There's something in those pills?"

"Yeah, but I don't know what."

"Oh my God! We need to get a nurse!"

"No, Mabel. We don't."

"Julio, we can't let her die like this!"

Nadine smiled at Mabel and shook her head yes as she whispered,

"S'ok."

"It's what she wants, Mabel. She can't take the pain anymore."

With tears flowing down her cheeks, Mabel kissed Nadine on the forehead and then went to Tommy and Julio's arms.

Nadine closed her eyes, foam formed around her mouth, and they heard the air leave her body.

Chapter 34 - Fricke Island

"Tommy Two Pockets. I didn't know you were still alive. Haven't seen you in like.... forever."

"Fiona. My God, look at you. After all these years, you're still a beauty. She looks great, doesn't she, Julio?"

"So right."

"Hello, Julio. Still hanging around with this reprobate?"

"Can't get rid of him, Fiona. God knows I've tried. Two Pockets is right, you look...... I don't know. Like....Like you could run the Boston Marathon."

At one time, Fiona Fricke Price, the owner of Fricke Island, the Fricke Island Marina, and Beanie's Sand Bar Grill weighed in at 320 lbs. At 6 foot 3, she was a formidable woman. Almost twenty years earlier, she and Matt Pervitch, Sissy's father, physically built the Marina. In the process, Fiona dropped over 100 lbs. and, with a different diet and exercise, lost another 50.

"I did."

"What do you mean you did?"

"Ran the Boston Marathon."

"What?"

"Yep, three times. My last one was four years ago. I'm getting the itch to do it again. Maybe next year."

Tommy Two Pockets
And the Posse of the Marsh

"You're going to run the Boston Marathon at your age?"

"Gee, Sissy, I thought you brought them out here to look at the cottage, not insult me." She said as she gave Tommy the stink eye.

"Sorry Fiona, I...I..."

"Oh, knock it off, Two Pockets. I'm beyond being offended by anything. I'm only too old when I say I am, and there are many ladies older than me there every year."

"Tommy can't help himself. He's a world-class smartass. Right Two Pockets?"

"So right, Julio."

"Well, Sissy here tells me you are in need of a new living arrangement. Apparently, "The Happiest Place Your Money Can Buy" doesn't suit you."

"Yeah, well, I didn't get along too well with the staff."

"That's nice to hear. Makes me just wanna hurry up and get your smart ass into the cottage. You won't be any trouble if we do this, will you?"

"No, Fiona, I'll be good as gold."

"What about you, little man?"

"So right."

"Ok, let's go take a look at the cottage. Hop in the cart, and let's take a ride."

Tommy Two Pockets
And the Posse of the Marsh

All four of them got into the three-row golf cart Fiona used to get from one end of the Island to the other. It was a beautiful ride back to the cottage at the south end of the island, not too far from Beanie's Sand Bar Grill. Beanie was a close family friend who was murdered by a motorcycle gang 18 years earlier. Once the grill was built, they named it after him. Since then, the grill has been operated by Fiona's twin sons, Floyd and Freddie Fricke, masters of the marsh. The grill is only open from May through September, leaving the twins the rest of the year to enjoy the wild area surrounding Fricke Island.

They passed through a stand of Birch and could see the channel leading out to Lake Erie on the west side of the Island. Julio smiled at the ca-coo of the blackbirds and the cicadas buzzing high in the trees. As they came to a stretch in the trail that closely bordered the marsh, Julio leaned forward and asked Fiona if she could slow down so he could enjoy the scenery.

"How bout I stop here for a few minutes, Julio?"

"So right."

Julio slowly got out of the cart and hobbled to the marsh's edge 20 feet away. The cattails and reeds swayed back and forth in the slight wind, making a broken whooshing sound. Panfish rose to the occasional unlucky bug that touched the water. A small flock of blue wing teal quickly filtered by, skipping over the water in their erratic flight. The sun shining through a large willow tree danced on the water. Julio took in a deep breath and held the slight fragrance of decay from the life cycle of the marsh. The familiar smell took him back through the special times in his life when everything seemed right. The memories of Black's Bay and the *Posse of the Marsh* and childhood protector and bud, Tommy Two Pockets. His head shook as he pulled a hanky out of his pocket and slowly wiped the tears rolling down his cheeks. The others left him alone. They recognized the time when a soul needs to be left to their own thoughts and emotions.

As he turned around to head back to the cart, Fiona asked him,

"Everything Ok Julio?"

He looked at her, nodded his head, and gave her a smile of total contentment.

"So....soooo...right."

"I had the twins check everything out after you called, Sissy. They said the fridge and stove still work fine, as do the toilet and shower. If you want a TV, they'll have to take the old antenna from the big house and bring it out here. I got cable last year, so I won't be using it. They didn't know about the small furnace, but we can get that checked out before fall."

"Now Fiona, you said nobody has lived here since 1969 after that big fella died."

"Yep, been empty for 18 yrs. That was D. A....... Remember him, Sissy?"

"Oh yeah, that was his name. He was a fixture at POPS when my brother worked there. All he ever said was, "yeeeeaaahhh."

Tommy Two Pockets
And the Posse of the Marsh

"From what I understand, I think I was the only one he talked to. Couldn't get him to shut up. But, as well as I knew him, I had no idea he was involved with drugs. That whole thing was a mess."

"Yeah, tell me about it."

In 1968 the Bricktown Motorcycle Club targeted high school kids with drugs that caused many to overdose resulting in several deaths. Sissy spent over a year in rehabilitation after a terrible evening gone wrong. D. A. was a part of the operation and died during the sweep when those responsible were arrested.

They stepped up onto the porch that looked out over Lake Erie, the sand bar, the marsh, and several small islands that marked the entrance to the channel that ran alongside the Island back to the marina. Julio shuffled over to an oversized bench and sat down. Tommy put his hand on his shoulder and said.

"What do you think, Julio?"

"Perfect. I think it's perfect."

"We haven't seen the inside yet, and we don't know how much it's gonna cost us."

"I don't need to see the inside. It's perfect."

"Well, let's go in anyway and check it out."

"You go. I wanna stay here."

"Well......Ok."

Tommy Two Pockets
And the Posse of the Marsh

"So, I know it's just a one-room cottage, but there's plenty of space, as you can see. I can get rid of that big bed and have the boys bring over a couple of twin-sized beds from the big house."

There was a well-stocked, fair-sized kitchen with a table and chairs. There was a living area with an oversized couch and recliner and a large area for two beds. A small bathroom with a shower was in one corner.

"I think we could make this work, Fiona, but I need to know how much you're asking for rent."

"How much can you afford Two Pockets?"

"Well, I've done a lot of figuring. Between food and I'm guessing about the utilities. I think we could swing two hundred a month if we're careful."

"I'll tell you what Two Pockets. I've been talking this over with the twins, and I think we've come up with something that will work for all of us. It was their idea. They're always looking for help with the grill. Do you think you could be available to fill in when they need some extra help? You know, clean tables, maybe help with dishes, sweep up. That kind of thing. Hard to get dependable help these days. It should be about 20 hours a week. Sometimes more. Sometimes less."

Tommy got a big smile on his face and said.

"Of course, I can. I even know how to cook."

"Well, we leave that to the twins. That's their specialty. Look, here's what we have in mind. You and Julio can live here for

Tommy Two Pockets
And the Posse of the Marsh

free during that time of year when the grill is open. When it's not, how does $75 a month sound? And don't worry about the utilities."

"Sounds great! But ah..........Julio, he can't work. He can hardly stand anymore."

"He can sit at the cash register, can't he?

"Course he can. He'd love it!"

"Then is it a deal?"

"Fiona, I could give you a big kiss!"

"Plant it right here, Two Pockets." Pointing to her lips.

He reached up and gave her a short kiss followed by a big hug,

"Thank you so much, Fiona. You're the best. Can you give me a minute to talk to Julio?"

"Take your time. Sissy, wanna get a coffee at the grill?"

"Sure."

"We'll be back later, Two Pockets."

Tommy sat next to Julio and watched as a big flock of redhead ducks landed near the mouth of the inlet. A blue heron slowly worked its way down the marsh's edge, occasionally poking its head in the water. A kingfisher sat not 30 feet from the porch, intently watching shiners move up and down a small creek. A chipmunk making its way across the porch railing was interrupted by a dragonfly landing in its path. Two small sailboats were making their way toward the mouth of the channel inlet, headed for the marina. In the distance, they could see a laker heading toward the Detroit River. The porch thermometer said 72 degrees and 57% humidity. It was partly cloudy with a slight breeze that swept through the porch. The smell of cedar dominated as Julio pulled out the handmade cherry pipe he made some 65 years earlier.

"Tell me it's affordable, Tommy."

"It's affordable Julio."

Julio closed his eyes and leaned into Tommy as he let out his last gasp of air.

Tommy Two Pockets
And the Posse of the Marsh

Chapter 35 - The Source

Tommy sat in his room at the home, trying to come to grips with what had happened earlier in the day. He had known Julio for as long as he could remember. His earliest memory was Julio walking around with a full load in his diaper. He was his best friend. He was a part of him and his identity. He felt empty. Confused. Directionless. They hadn't been apart since the end of WWII. They served on merchant ships together for roughly 20 years before Tommy bought a commercial fishing boat. They became Lake Erie commercial fishermen, plying that meager trade for another 20 years.

As Julio's health began failing, it became apparent to Tommy that they had to get off the water and into a place that could care for his needs. He sold the boat and used that money to supplement what little they got from Social Security so they could go to the Mouillee Rest Home. That money was almost gone, so a venue change was attractive to Tommy. But without Julio......

He spent the night in the chair, looking out over the marsh and dozing off now and then. He skipped breakfast and was just getting ready to shower when there was a knock at his door. It was "Renta"-Hank with the Brownstown Police Chief Rudy Pervitch.

"Tommy, you know Rudy, don't ya? He'd like to have a word with you."

"Rudy. I thought you'd be retired by now."

"No. I don't plan to. It's a pretty good gig."

"How's your brother Matt?"

Tommy Two Pockets
And the Posse of the Marsh

"Well not too bad. He had a heart attack last year. It really knocked the wind out of his sails. But the doctor says he's doing real good. He can get a bit cranky, but he always was. I don't think that the low fat, low carb diet Joyce has him on helps his demeanor."

"Hey, if you two are gonna have old home week, I'm outta here."

"Thanks for bringing me back, Hank."

"Yeah, better get back before the Griz misses ya."

"Up yours Two Pockets."

"Mr. Two Pockets to you, Renta-Hank."

"What's that all about?"

"Aw.....the guy's a jerk."

"Say. Sorry to hear about Julio. I know you guys were a team. He was a good guy."

"Even when you arrested him?"

"And you. Minor stuff. Nothing personal. And that was a long time ago."

"Yeah, I know."

"Look mmm....Julio is why I'm here."

"Ok. What's up?"

Tommy Two Pockets
And the Posse of the Marsh

"What do you know about these?"

"About what?"

Rudy handed him a picture showing a small clear package with three pills. Red, white, and blue.

"Do you know what these are, Tommy?"

"Ah........no."

But he did know. They were the same pills that Nadine had taken to end her life.

"Why are you asking me?"

"These were found on Julio. So you don't know what they are?"

"No. What are they?"

"Well, they're suicide pills. We've seen this little cocktail in the area for the past two years but have been unable to track down where they come from."

"Are you saying Julio committed suicide?"

"No, there's no indication that Julio took any pills. He just had them on him. Look, I'm not supposed to say anything, but it appears that Julio died of liver failure, according to the ME. His family doctor confirmed this. He said Julio had a massive growth on his liver caused by a piece of lead that had been in his system for years. He said something about Julio being shot with a shotgun, and the doctor at the time couldn't find the pellet. You know anything about that?"

Tommy Two Pockets
And the Posse of the Marsh

"Ah.....yeah, that's why he limped. We ah..........we were kids. Julio was shot and....and.....that son of a bitch!"

"Who? Who's a son of a bitch?"

"Otis Pies. Otis shot him. That son of a bitch killed one more person. He killed Julio."

"Otis Pies? I remember that name. He was that woodcutter from Black's Bay that kidnapped girls and took them out to that hidden island in the marsh, right?"

"Yep."

"Dad told me the stories when we were growing up. Didn't Otis shoot Julio on that Island where they found all those bodies?"

"Yeah. Crow Island."

"Dad said you kids were there when Otis was shot, but they never found the body."

"No. We all worried about that for years but never heard from him again, so we figured he must have died in the marsh. No one would ever find him if he died in one of them potholes or got caught in the goop in the bottom of a marsh pond."

"Hmm.... I remember Dad telling me you were a hero."

"I don't know about any of that."

"Well, that's what he said, and if the old man said it, then it had to be true."

Tommy Two Pockets
And the Posse of the Marsh

"I suppose."

"He talked a lot about Black's Bay and how it was a great place to grow up."

"We had a lot of adventures with Sonny. Wish he was still around."

"Yeah......yeah, me too."

"So, any idea how Julio got his hands on those pills?"

"No. What's in 'em?"

"Not too sure. The lab says that the red and white pills are tranquilizers, and the blue is a hyped-up speedball. Now we understand a friend of yours,... let's see, what's her name?"

He thumbed through his notebook.

"Here it is, Nadine. Nadine Sharbinaeu. It looks like she had access to those pills and used them. I understand you were with her the night she died. Did you give them to her?"

"What? Me? Why would I do that?"

"But you were with her when she died."

"Well yeah, I was there.......but I didn't give her the pills."

"Did you see them?"

"Ah....maybe."

"Did you or did you not see the pills before she took them?"

Tommy Two Pockets
And the Posse of the Marsh

"Wait a minute. What kind of trouble am I in?"

"Right now? None. So you saw the pills before she took them?"

"Yeah....yeah, I guess I did."

"Did you help her?"

Tommy went to his chair, sat down, and looked out the window.

"Tommy, I need an answer. Don't make me have to take you to the station and sort this out. Did you help her take the pills?"

"Damn. Yeah....yeah, I helped her take the blue pill."

"Did you know what it was for?"

"Just before I put it in her mouth, she told me what was going on. If you could have seen her and known what she had gone through and Otis and everything. I didn't argue with her and.......I put the last one in her mouth for her."

"Otis? Nadine?......That Nadine?"

"Yeah, that, Nadine."

"Oh....... So who clsc was there?"

"Am I in trouble now?"

"Who else was there?"

248

Tommy Two Pockets
And the Posse of the Marsh

"Just me and Julio."

"And Mabel...... right?"

"Yeah, Mabel, but she didn't do anything."

"How much trouble am I in?"

"None that I can tell. I'll have to make a report and see where it goes from there."

"Can I ask a question?"

"Sure."

"Jimmy Cooper. Same thing?"

"Yeah. How did you know?"

"We heard about the foam in the mouth thing."

"Foam in the mouth thing?"

"Yeah, it happens when you OD."

"I don't know about that. But yes, Jimmy Cooper got his hands on the pills and so have several others here at the home and in the surrounding community."

"Really? Anybody I know?"

Rudy scrunched his face and looked at Tommy.

"Can't leave this room. Promise."

Tommy Two Pockets
And the Posse of the Marsh

"Sure, I promise."

"Lips."

"What? Holy Crap. Lips? Why would he do that?"

"Well, from what I gather from the family, he had all kinds of health issues and was in and out of the hospital numerous times. He couldn't get around very well anymore, his eyesight was about gone, and he was just diagnosed with cancer. So I guess it was more than he wanted to handle."

"Family know?"

"Unfortunately, I had to tell them. I need to find out where they're coming from. Funny thing. I ran into him about a month ago. He was sitting in a wheelchair just inside his room at the hospital, waiting to be discharged. We started talking, and so I pulled up a chair. You know we talked, or I listened, for about an hour. You know what he talked about? Black's Bay, you, Julio, Lumpy, my dad, the Posse.......Otis."

"What did he say?"

"Said he had the greatest adventures of his life growing up in Blacks Bay. Said he'd give anything to go back there and live that life again. Said it was the freest he ever felt."

"But, he was a war hero and everything. I'd have thought that was his biggest adventure."

"I had the same thought and asked him about it. He said months of drudgery piled onto monotonous months of drudgery with about an hour of excitement. Nah, he said. He loved Black's Bay, and that's why he never left. Said he did

250

Tommy Two Pockets
And the Posse of the Marsh

that so his kids could have the same freedom he had growing up. They said he was a really good father."

"That's funny. He was such a goofball as a kid. So tell me, Rudy, what's gonna happen to the person supplying those pills?"

"Well, they'd be arrested. It's a felony."

"But, whoever it is, is just trying to help people with no more hope. People are tired of living. Their bodies are giving out, and so are they. What's the harm?"

"I know what you're saying, Two Pockets, but what if whoever is doing this starts encouraging people to off themselves because they're sad or lonely. That's not good. If this person thinks they can play God, I don't think that's good for the community."

"Yeah, I guess, but I'll tell ya, Rudy, there are lots of people in this place who would probably take that option over sitting around all day with drool coming down their mouth and a full load in their drawers. Comes down to it, if I'm in that position, I want the option!"

"I get it, Two Pockets. It's a tough one. I don't know what the right answer is. I just know what the law is, and I've got to do my job."

"I know Rudy. I know."

Chapter 36 - The Next Week

The following Tuesday, they held an outdoor funeral for Dory's father, Gus Perkins, followed by one for 5x5. Most of the 280 residents of the village of Black's Bay attended as well as a few others that made their way there via boat. The road and small bridge with the only land access to Black's Bay would be out of commission for the foreseeable future.

On Wednesday, word spread around town that a reporter, Ralph Randazzo from the Monroe Gazette, had shown up by boat to report the previous week's events. He spent three days at Black's Bay and got the royal treatment from everyone in town. On the first day, he interviewed Chief Clark, Doc Landrith, Father Mac, Old Man Black, Red Thomkins, and the old "part-time whenever they needed him jailer," Martin Swenson. The interview with Martin was the most challenging, as Martin played up his hearing problem.

Ralph spent the second day with the *Posse of the Marsh* in Kramer's shed. Mrs. Kramer provided sandwiches, apples, and lemonade. There were many stories for him to report, and he planned to submit them to his editor to be published over several Sunday editions. Maybe someday, he thought, turn it into a book.

At the end of the day, he asked the *Posse of the Marsh* to gather for a picture in front of Black's Fish House.

Dory was recovering quickly from getting shot in the rear but taking her father's death pretty hard. She didn't have much to say to the reporter but enjoyed her kinship with the other Posse members.

Tommy Two Pockets
And the Posse of the Marsh

Mabel complained about the constant itchiness of her back under the liniment-soaked bandages, but the Doc said she was healing pretty well and didn't have an infection. He credited Lumpy's quick thinking with the mud poultice.

Tommy had worse injuries from the cuts from the thorn bushes than he did from the single pellet that went in and out of the side of his leg above the knee cap.

It appeared Julio got the worst of it. Of the three pellets, Doc Landrith could only get one out. Another one buried itself in the socket where his femur joins the hip. Doc Landrith told him it could give him trouble for the rest of his life. The last one was deep in his organs on the right side of his back, just under the rib cage. The Doc was not able to locate it when he probed for it. Julio seemed to take it in stride despite what happened to him and didn't want too much of a fuss. He had to sit for the picture.

While the Posse was busy with the reporter, the futile search continued for Otis Pics. Using tracking dogs, they followed the trail as best they could but lost him deep in the marsh. With the amount of blood they found, they assumed he was most likely lying dead in one of the many potholes to be found in the marsh. They continued to keep a vigilant watch out for Otis in case he survived. But as the days, weeks, and then years went by, doors were left unlocked, and the safe, secure feeling only a small village can provide returned to Black's Bay.

On Friday, Chief Clark, Doc Landrith, and Johnny Cecil met the Monroe County Sheriff with three deputies at Black's Fishhouse dock. Along with Ricky Randazzo, they loaded up in canoes and made their way to Crow Island. With the information they obtained from Nadine Kramer, they found the remains of several bodies in shallow graves behind the cabin. One of the bodies wore an old farmwife's bonnet. Doc recognized it as belonging to Otis's wife, Belinda.

Nadine Kramer wasn't able to shed any more light on the identities of the bodies other than one she knew as Wilda. She wasn't sure about the last name but thought it was Yedrich or something like that. The County Sheriff confirmed that a Wilda Yederic was on file as a missing person for the past 2-½ years. Nadine saw Otis beat her to death when she dropped a plate of sweet rolls. This happened shortly after Nadine was abducted and taken to the island.

Nadine had no idea where she was the entire time and didn't see or hear any person besides Wilda and Otis. She was beaten regularly and figured that with the severity of the beatings getting worse, it was just a matter of time before he brought in a new victim, and she was killed.

She only stayed in Black's Bay one day before leaving for the hospital at the University of Michigan in an attempt to heal her back. Old Man Black had to take her and Mrs. Kramer by boat to Monroe, where they caught the train to Ann Arbor. She was put in a body cast. After she was released three months later, she went to Escanaba, Michigan, to stay with her Aunt. She needed some time away from Black's Bay.

On Saturday night, a banquet sponsored by Black's Fishhouse was held at St. Henry's to honor the *Posse of the Marsh*. The $100 reward was matched by Old Man Black and equally divided among the seven children. Lumpy didn't think it was fair to go with the original plan and give it all to him because, in the end, they all helped, and all could use the money. It was a wonderful night for the group as they sat at the head table and were allowed all the fried fish, corn on the cob, and apple pie they could eat.

As Tommy sat watching his friends, he felt pride and sadness for what they experienced. He marveled at the change in Lumpy. The bully turned hero, protector.......friend. Lumpy from the other end of the table looked at Tommy, gave a little smile, slightly bobbed his head up and down, and wiped a single tear that trickled down his cheek. It was a thank you. Lumpy was saying thank you for saving me. Tommy got up, walked down to the end of the table, and from behind, put his arms around Lumpy's neck and whispered in his ear,

"Yeah......You saved me too."

The Kramers insisted that Lumpy stay with them for as long as he wanted, despite Otis's actions. Lumpy got to see what a real father was like. It was the beginning of a good life.

Chapter 37 - Enough

The Posse went to Cap's after lunch to talk about a service for Julio. He would be cremated that day, and Cap knew they needed to keep Tommy's mind busy. They all knew that a full-blown funeral was out of the question. They didn't think Julio would want the dining room reserved for a service open to everyone. The discussion was getting nowhere when Mabel finally said,

"The bench. Let's go down to the bench and have a service there."

"You mean the one in the lobby? That's a silly place for a funeral."

"No Suds, ya dope. His bench. The one he and Tommy built by the marsh. Where he went to get away from everybody."

"There's a bench by the marsh? I didn't know that."

"Julio and I took you fishing down there. You caught a nice channel cat, and the kitchen wouldn't fix it for you. Man, did you throw a fit."

"When was that, Tommy?"

Tommy looked around at everybody and then the puzzled look in Suds' eyes.

"Never mind Suds, it must have been someone else."

"Probably. I think that's something I'd remember."

"Yeah, that's something you'd remember."

256

Tommy Two Pockets
And the Posse of the Marsh

Mabel started a list of who to invite.

"Let's see. I've got the Posse, Marvella, Frank, Miss Sissy…"

Cap and Tommy both said at the same time.

"Gertie Does."

"Of course, Gertie."

"He was Catholic. Think we can get Father Burt there?"

"I don't know, Mooch. He hasn't been to church for years."

"Whad'ya mean, Tommy? He always went to the early morning mass Father Burt had every Sunday morning. I don't remember him ever missing."

"Really, Mooch? There's an early mass on Sunday?"

"Yep, 6 in the morning every Sunday. We call it the pajama service."

"And Julio went? Huh. I never knew that."

"I'll call Father Burt. When are we gonna do it?"

"Ok Mooch, that's good. You call him. We can't do it Saturday; we've got Lip's funeral. How does Monday sound, say 10 in the morning?"

"I like it, Cap. I think Julio would too."

"Ok Mabel if you would spread the word. Mooch, call Father Burt. I'll arrange for something to toast with and maybe a little something to eat. Maybe a brunch. I think I can get the staff to bring some chairs down. We can make this real nice for him."

"Sounds good Cap."

"Now, I think it's time to head over to the east porch. We have a special treat today. The tall sailing ship USS Niagara out of Erie, Pennsylvania, comes through within the hour. She's heading to Port Huron to participate in the Mackinaw run. So let's get going. I certainly don't want to miss it."

As the five of them walked down the hall, they could see people standing outside the entrance to the porch.

"What's going on, Marvella?"

"It's closed, Cap! Look!"

"What?"

"Read the sign on the door."

"The East Porch is permanently closed for construction. Construction? What construction? There must be a mistake. Let me talk to Ms. Haverhill. I'm sure this is a mistake."

"I'm going with you, Cap."

"Me too, Cap."

"Ok, Tommy. Mabel, let's go, but please let me do the talking."

"Sure."

Tommy Two Pockets
And the Posse of the Marsh

They saw Renta-Hank standing outside of Ms. Haverhill's door as they got to the lobby.

"She's not in, Captain Dougherty."

"Where is she?"

Hank looked at the door and back to Cap.

"She said to tell you she's not in."

"Ok, you've told me. You've done your job. Good man, Hank. Now please step aside."

Hank walked away as Cap knocked on the door. There was no answer, so he knocked again. As he was knocking for the 3rd time, the door opened. Ms. Haverhill glared at Hank, who was back by the front entrance at his station.

"Can I help you, Mr. Dougherty?"

"That's Captain Dougherty."

"Whatever. What do you want?"

"The east porch is closed, and I have a lecture there this afternoon."

"Oh, one of your unauthorized lectures?"

"What do you mean by unauthorized lectures, Ms. Haverhill?"

"Do you see your lectures on any schedule put out by the home? No, that's because you decided to do this

259

independently and never turned in the paperwork to make this an official Mouillee Rest Home event. It is unapproved and unsanctioned."

"An official Mouillee Rest Home event? Unapproved? Unsanctioned? Paperwork? Are you serious, Ms. Haverhill? A group of my friends and I gather 3 to 4 times a week to discuss maritime traffic. We have been doing this for almost seven years. You know this. We don't do any harm. We don't require any staff. We don't cost the home a penny in doing this. Again, are you serious?"

"Quite serious."

"Why didn't you give me some notification?"

"You mean for your unauthorized lectures?"

"You know we hold them. What construction is going on? How long before we have access to the East Porch again?"

"I'm afraid, Mr. Dougherty, you will never have access to the porch again."

"What? And why not?"

"Because the east porch is being turned into four more studio apartments, as is the west porch."

"You're doing what?"

"You heard me."

"Why?"

Tommy Two Pockets
And the Posse of the Marsh

"I would think that would be very obvious, Mr. Dougherty. We want to expand where we can, and this is an easy way to do it."

"At the expense of the people that already live here?"

"Oh, but it's not going to cost the current residents anything for the new construction. In fact it will save them money in the long run because we will have more residents to help offset overhead costs."

"But you are taking away an amenity that the people enjoy. If you paid attention, you would know that people mill about on the porches almost all the time. It is not only a place where we meet to discuss the ships that pass by, but the porches are a main social hub in our little community. What are we supposed to do now?"

"We've thought of that, Mr. Dougherty. We have decided to turn the theater into a lounge where people can go and sit and visit."

Mabel got between Cap and the Griz.

"Wait a minute. Are you taking away our movie privileges too? You can't do that. For some people here, it's the big event of the week!!"

"To be honest, we have talked about this for some time, and were having a hard time making a decision. But you can thank Two Pockets here for pushing the issue over the edge. And by the way, what are you still doing here, Two Pockets?"

"Mr. Tupoc to you, Griz. I've got a few more days, and I'll be out of this miserable shithole."

Tommy Two Pockets
And the Posse of the Marsh

"Watch your language, Two Pockets."

"Bite me Griz! And what do you mean I pushed it over the edge?"

"Well, that porn movie you showed was the last straw. After all, we lost a resident because of it."

"Lost a resident? What are you talking about?"

"Jimmy Cooper died because he got excited seeing that disgusting pornographic film you were responsible for."

"You are a dumbass, Griz. Do you think he died because he got an enlarged willy watching a skin flick? He committed suicide, you idiot!!!"

"He what?"

"He commi............."

Tommy stopped short when he realized he had said too much.

"You said he committed suicide. What would make you say something like that, Two Pockets?"

"Nothing. Never mind."

"No. Why did you say that?"

"Look, you need to talk to the cops about that."

"The cops? Have you been talking to the police about this?"

Tommy Two Pockets
And the Posse of the Marsh

"Well, they've been talking to me."

"Why would they be talking to you?"

"If you want to know why, call Chief Rudy. Let him tell you all about it."

"Oh, I will. I most definitely will."

"Ok, Ms. Haverhill. To be absolutely clear, you have no intention of leaving the east porch alone."

"That is correct, Captain Dougherty."

"Alright, Ms. Haverhill. As you wish. Come on, everyone, let's leave Ms. Haverhill alone. I'm sure she has more important things to do than listen to our complaints."

"But, Cap!"

"No Mabel let's go. You too Tommy."

Captain Dougherty walked away with a smile on his face.

Chapter 38 - Lips Service

St. Henry's was packed when they arrived on the very old, small Mouillee Rest Home bus. Sissy didn't bother to ask permission to use it. She just took it.

Waiting for them were her parents, Matt and Joyce Pervitch, along with Sissy's brother Mickey and his wife, Paula. Matt and Joyce were co-owners of the Fricke Island Marina and lived in a house they built on the island.

Mickey was a part-time game warden with the Michigan Department of Natural Resources while running a full-time hunting/fishing guide service out of the Fricke Island Marina. Paula worked part-time at the Marina but spent most of her time keeping house for Mickey and their two children, Sonny 12, and Cindy, 14. They also built a small home on the island near his parents, allowing Matt and Joyce plenty of Grandparent time.

"Tommy, you know my parents, Matt and Joyce, don't you?"

"Oh sure, Sissy. Been a while, but yes, I know them. I hope you don't mind me saying so, Matt, but you're still a looker, Joyce."

"You're too kind."

"No, you're too pretty. And Mickey? I haven't seen you since... I guess since you first became a warden, and we'd run into each other out on the lake. Are you still doing that? Harassing honest commercial fishermen trying to make a living?"

Tommy Two Pockets
And the Posse of the Marsh

"Come on. I was pretty easy on you, Mr. Tupoc. But yeah, I still do it part-time, but mostly I run the guide service."

"I heard about that. Maybe I can talk you into taking me out to catch some perch sometime."

"I'd love to, especially since you're going to be living on the Island. You still are, aren't you? I mean after Julio......."

"Yeah, Julio....No, I'm still planning on it. In fact, Sissy's going to take me out on Tuesday. I'm sure I'll see you around."

"Yeah. Freddie and Floyd said you'd be working with them part-time. I thought if you have too much time on your hand, I could use some part-time help too."

"Wait a minute, Mickey. I was going to ask him the same thing."

"Wow, nice to be wanted for a change. Thanks Matt. I'll tell ya, the busier I am, the better."

"Oh, we'll keep you busy!"

"How long did Lips work for you at the marina?"

"Leonard? Gee, I don't know, 10 yrs? I'll tell ya. He was a Godsend when we first opened the marina. Wasn't anything he couldn't do. Best boat mechanic I ever saw. I learned a lot from him. This will be a tough funeral for me.....he....yeah."

"Me too, Matt. He was a goofy kid, but he was a good friend. Just like your dad. I'll tell ya, Sonny would be proud of what you've done."

"Hmm....I hope so. Now that you're going to be on Fricke Island, maybe you can tell me about when you were kids. Joyce is a great cook!"

"I'd like that Matt. I really would. Thanks."

Captain Dougherty walked over.

"Sorry to break this up, Tommy, but the funeral director is looking for us."

"Ok. See you guys later."

The funeral director, Tony Ford, gathered everyone around him and explained their duties as pallbearers.

"Gentlemen and Miss Mabel, this is how we will do this. You are the official pallbearers; however, I will not let anyone get hurt. So these four gentlemen that work for me will do most of the heavy lifting. Do not strain yourself. There is no reason to. The tough part will be carrying the casket up the ten steps into the church and then out the back of the Church for the burial after the service. Now keep in mind that these four men can do it easily by themselves. So I ask you to just put your hand on one of the handles and let them do the rest. Is that clear? Once we reach the top of the stairs, we'll place the casket on the rolling table, and from there, you will be the only ones holding the handles. I will be pushing the casket from behind. Everyone understand?"

"Yes. You won't have any heroics from us. Right, Suds?"

"Aye aye, Cap."

Tommy Two Pockets
And the Posse of the Marsh

Typically, funerals were the main social events in this small, tight-knit community. However, the town folks were genuinely there to pay their respects to a long-time community fixture and friend of all. This same group would respectfully meet again next week for Nadine's funeral.

They walked the casket down the aisle to the front of the church, preceded by seven members of the Navy Honor Guard made up of Navy reserve and retired Navy personnel.

Leonard's granddaughter Lisa sang the old hymn "*It Is Well*" accompanied by her brother Andy on the classical guitar. Both were accomplished musicians. You could hear a lot of sniffling and nose blowing when the hymn was over.

After Father Chinavare read the liturgy, he gave a fair and detailed account of Lip's life. Included in the tribute was mention of his time growing up on Black's Bay.

"I thoroughly enjoyed my time talking with Leonard or Lips, as most everyone called him. I was especially intrigued with his accounts of his adventures as a child with the *Posse of the Marsh*. In his notes, he wanted me to mention three people that he thought would be here today and how important they were to his childhood. So I will ask if these people are here and if you are, would you please stand up? Mabel Pies, Julio Garza, and Tommy "Two Pockets" Tupoc. Ok. I see two of you here. You must be Mabel, and are you, Tommy?"

Tommy cleared his throat and said.

"Yes, father. Hmm.... Julio passed away last.......last.....Julio passed away last week."

Tommy Two Pockets
And the Posse of the Marsh

"Oh I see. I am so sorry." He said as he crossed himself. "Leonard asked me to read this at the funeral."

"There are two periods of my life I wish I could live over. When my kids were growing up and when I grew up on Black's Bay. I hope when I am in heaven, I will see Sonny and Lumpy and, at some point, be joined by Dory, Julio, Mabel, and Two Pockets. What adventures we'll have."

At the end of the service, they moved outside to the Church Cemetery. After a brief internment message, there was a 21-gun salute, playing of Taps, and the folding of the flag presented to the family by Senior Chief Petty Officer Springstead.

Chapter 39 - Senior Chief Petty Officer Springstead

As usual, the parish ladies went overboard preparing for the funeral lunch, leaving plenty of leftovers for the LaRue family to take home. Tommy and the others filled their plates with green bean casserole, corn, scalloped potatoes, Swedish meatballs, ham, and everyone's favorite, Sister Lou's hot cross buns.

As Tommy was digging into his second piece of cherry pie, he heard.

"Mr. Tupoc.......sir."

He looked up and saw a man in a Navy Uniform. Tommy recognized him from the honor guard. He looked at the insignia and his nametag, held out his hand, and said,

"Yes...Senior Chief Petty Officer uh...Springstead, that's me."

He slowly took Tommy's hand and stared into Tommy's eyes. After a brief awkward moment, Tommy said,

"Can I help you?"

"Mmmmm.......Well, yes......Do you have a minute to talk?"

"Sure, the bus back to the home isn't leaving for a while. Have a seat."

"Could we go somewhere quiet?"

Tommy Two Pockets
And the Posse of the Marsh

Tommy squinted his eyes and looked around him, then back up at the Navy man.

"Mmm.....I guess. Why? What's this about? I'm not going back to the Navy. I was dishonorably discharged 40 years ago, and they can't make me go back."

"Oh, ha. Yeah, no, nothing like that. I've just got some questions I'd like to ask you."

"You can't do it here?"

"I'd rather not. It's ah.....private."

"Well..... ok then. Let's go back up to the sanctuary. Shouldn't be anyone there."

While they walked up the stairs, Tommy asked if he was still in the service.

"Yes. Just went from active duty to reserve."

"How long were on active?"

"Thirty years."

"Wow, good for you. So you went in.... when.... '57?"

"Yeah, that's right."

"See any action?"

"Nam, I was aboard the carrier USS Midway."

"The Midway? So you saw the Saigon Evacuation."

Tommy Two Pockets
And the Posse of the Marsh

"Only from the ship. Most of the time, I was below the flight deck, but it was pretty hectic."

"I'll bet."

They went to the back of the sanctuary and sat facing each other on two ushers' chairs.

"Ok. So what's up?"

"It's just.......well......."

The Seaman looked around the room and pulled at his collar.

"Are you ok? You look a little flushed."

"Sorry.... Hmmmm..... It's just that this came as a big surprise today........Hearing your name."

"My name. Why's that?"

"Well. I thought you were dead. I thought you were killed in action during World War II."

"Ah...No, but I know many people who would like to see me dead. Why would you think I'm dead, and why would you care? Who are you? What do you want?"

"Because....."

He put his head down, and when he looked back up at Tommy, tears were rolling down his cheeks.

"You wanna tell me what's going on here?"

271

Tommy Two Pockets
And the Posse of the Marsh

"My mom told me you were dead. She said you were killed aboard the destroyer Hammond during the battle of Midway."

"Well, the ship went down, but I was only in the water for maybe half an hour before we were picked up. But, wait a minute, why would your...... I don't get it."

"I remember the day Mom got a telegram from the Navy saying you were dead."

"Your Mom got a letter from the Navy? What? Who's your mom, and why would she.......Who are you?"

"Alex."

"Alex? Ok Alex Springstead, what's that got............"

The light was starting to come on for Tommy.

"Springstead is my adopted name."

Tommy looked at him with his bottom lip shaking, trying to recognize a four-year-old in the face before him.

"My God..........Alex? My Alex? My son..........Alex?!"

Alex nodded his head.

"I think so."

Tommy grabbed the sides of the chair and started to shake while tears slowly flowed out of his eyes. His arms then fell to the sides, and he went limp as he fell back into the chair. He then sat up and reached across and touched the face of a boy he once knew and loved.

Tommy Two Pockets
And the Posse of the Marsh

"This isn't a joke? This is for real?"

"Yes."

They stared at each other in the quiet of the church, each struggling for their next words.

"You have Meg's cheekbones. But why? Why did your mother run out on me? Is she still alive? Trudy? What about Trudy? My letters were returned, and I stopped getting anything from Meg. Why? Why?"

Alex took out his hanky, wiped his face, composed himself, and sat up straight in his chair.

"Ok. You have to remember I was four years old, so I can only tell you what I remember. Trudy? Who's Trudy?"

"Trudy, your sister."

Alex looked off into the distance and then finally said.

"Was that her name? I barely remember a little sister and calling her sister, but I couldn't remember her name....... I'm sorry. I don't know what happened to her or mom."

"Nothing? Don't you know anything? How did you end up with the last name Springstead?"

"Well, let's see. This is all I know. The day Mom got the telegram from the Navy was a tough day. Then, I don't know. Hmm....not too long after that, I woke up in the middle of the night, and there was a man in the kitchen with Mom. She told me to go back to bed, and that was the last time I saw her. Three or four days later, some ladies came to the house and took us to an orphanage in Detroit. The Evangelical Orphanage, I remember that. A few months later, I was taken to the Springstead's in Rockwood, and they adopted me. I never saw my sister after they took me to their home. I don't know what happened to her. When I was in high school, they told me that I was adopted, but I had already figured out I was adopted. I remember asking my adoptive parents about my sister. I remembered bits and pieces like you taking us on a picnic and catching sunfish. And I remember my sister getting bit by a big dog on the leg and screaming and going to the doctor and getting stitches.......We got ice cream on the way home."

"I remember that. We were at Black's Bay, and a stray came over where we were having a picnic. The dog grabbed something, and Trudy grabbed it too. Got her pretty good before I could get to 'em. Scared the hell out of me. What did they say about Trudy?"

"They didn't know anything about her. I remember Dad getting in touch with the home, but they wouldn't tell him anything."

"This is too much. I'm getting dizzy."

"Put your head between your knees and take deep breaths. It'll pass."

"Yeah, yeah, I'm alright. I just. Geez. This is a shock.."

"For me too."

"I was discharged in '46, and I hired a PI to find you, but he didn't turn up anything. If you guys were in an orphanage or were adopted, that should have been easy enough to find

Tommy Two Pockets
And the Posse of the Marsh

out. That shyster. All this time, I thought Meg had just left me. Looks like she left us all. I don't know what I did wrong. What I did wrong was going into the Navy after Pearl. I could've..... I should've stayed. I didn't have to go. I was a merchant seaman. I was exempt from the draft. But Meg and I both agreed I had a duty. Do you know who this man was that you saw with Meg?"

"No. I never saw him before or since."

"Did you hear his name? What did he look like?"

Alex closed his eyes and thought.

"Mmmmm.......No. No name. I remember his hands. They were real big, and I think he looked kind of old, but I'm not sure. He just looked at me, smiled, and said something."

"What did he say?"

"I don't really remember, but let me think about it. It was so long ago and I was only about four."

Tommy stood up and stared off into the distance. Then mumbled,

"No, it can't be. He died in the marsh. How could he be alive then? Would have been in his 60's? 70's? That can't be."

"Who? Who are you talking about?"

"Otis. Otis Pies."

"Otis Pies. I know that name. He was the woodcutter from Black's Bay?"

Tommy Two Pockets
And the Posse of the Marsh

"Yeah, that's right. How do you know about him?"

"I remembered my last name was Tupoc, and I remember mom calling you Tommy. Tommy Tupoc. A while back, I wanted to find out something about you, and I have this friend, a reporter Ralph Randazzo. I was talking to him about it, and he said he remembered an article his grandfather did on some kids from Black's Bay back in the 20s. Said he got some journalistic award for it. Ralph was able to dig up the articles from the Monroe Gazette, and I read them. I remember they said you were a hero. I was proud to know that about you. But I remember the woodcutter and what he did. What? Do you think it was him?"

"I don't see how.........God, I hope not."

"Mr. Tupoc, Sissy sent me looking for you. She's ready to take the bus back to the rest home. Are you alright?"

"Mickey, I'd like you to meet my........."

Tommy broke down in tears as Alex put his arms around him.

"I'm his son Alex."

"Oh, I didn't know he had a son."

"I didn't know I had a father."

"I'll go tell Sissy to wait a bit."

"Could I give you a ride back?"

Tommy Two Pockets
And the Posse of the Marsh

Tommy stepped back, wiped his eyes, and pulled out a hanky.

"Ah....yeah sure, that would be great."

They took their time returning to the Mouillee Rest Home while Tommy pumped Alex full of questions. He found out that Alex lived in Brighton, a few hours away. He was a widower. His wife died three years earlier from cervical cancer. He regretted that he spent most of his career on long assignments. Tommy found out he had a granddaughter at Eastern Michigan University studying to become a teacher, and a grandson, Alex Jr., a warrant officer on board the USS Dwight D. Eisenhower.

Tommy took it all in and couldn't get enough. With each new revelation about the family he didn't know he had, he pulled out the by now, well used hanky.

After Tommy took Alex to meet Mabel, they went back to his room, where they spent the next four hours talking. Alex suggested that Tommy come live with him in Brighton, but Tommy thought it would be good to get to know each other better before they entertained something like that. Besides, Tommy was looking forward to his new adventure on Fricke Island. Alex said he would see him next weekend on the Island. In the meantime, he would try to remember more.

It was a strange day for Tommy. It was a good day. He hardly slept that night.

Chapter 40 - Change

It was a nice morning for Julio's short service at the marsh pond bench. Seventy degrees and low humidity. A slight breeze forced the marsh reeds and cattails into their mystic chant. Mixed with the sounds of the pond creatures, it was a chorus Julio would sit and listen to in a trance-like state for hours.

Several people spoke, including Tommy, who choked his way through a brief talk. He reminisced about their time as kids on Black's Bay and their years together on Tommy's small commercial fishing boat. He finished by saying,

"So right."

At the end of the service, a drake Mallard with a noticeable limp walked through the middle of the small group on its way to the pond. Mabel nudged Tommy in the side and pointed.

"Julio's here."

Everyone heard her and had a good laugh.

Captain Dougherty had arranged for a nice brunch through the kitchen, which was highly unusual but indicative of the type of influence he had at the Home.

Sissy stopped by at the beginning of the service but was called away by Renta-Hank.

As the tables and chairs were being carted up the hill by staff members, Tommy sat on the bench and started drifting back to the past. So much had changed in such a short time. Lips,

278

Tommy Two Pockets
And the Posse of the Marsh

Julio, and tomorrow his new home on Fricke Island. Add to that Saturday's surprise, and he felt overwhelmed, yet excited, about his new prospects.

"Come on, Tommy, walk me back up the hill. I'm not that steady anymore."

"Yeah ok. But we're not going steady, Mabel."

"In your dreams, Two Pockets. In your dreams."

As the two old friends walked up the hill arm in arm, they said little but,

"I love you, Tommy Two Pockets. You know? Like a brother."

"I feel the same way, Mabel. I love me too."

"Smart Ass."

"Yeah...........but I love you. Always have. Always will."

"Oh...... you're going to make me cry!"

Tommy planned to spend the rest of the day packing up for the move to Fricke Island. He could hardly wait, but knew he would miss his friends at the home. One by one, they came to say their goodbyes. He told everyone that he'd throw a BBQ party and have them all out to see his new digs once he was settled in.

Finally, Cap came to see him.

"Tommy, is it true what I was told about your son Alex?"

Tommy Two Pockets
And the Posse of the Marsh

"Yeah Cap, it's true."

"That's got to be a real shocker. I remember Meg. What a gem she was. What about her and your daughter?"

"I wish I knew. I don't know how to go about finding out. All I know is Trudy went to the Evangelical Orphanage with Alex, and Meg ran off with some man with big hands."

"The Evangelical Orphanage. Hmmm. It's the Evangelical Home for Children and Aged now. I've been a patron for years. Some of my best deckhands came from there. Hmmm....."

Cap rubbed his chin and walked around Tommy's tiny room.

"What is it, Cap?"

"Well. I still know somebody there. Would you object to my nosing around a little bit and see if I can convince them to open some records?"

"Can you do that? Can they? Is that legal?"

"Probably not, but I can ask. I have some influence there. After all, my niece runs the place."

"Your niece runs it?"

"Yes. Good girl. Let me see what I can do."

"Cap, that would be great."

"No promises, but let me give her a call this afternoon."

Tommy Two Pockets
And the Posse of the Marsh

"Wow. You're the best Cap. The best."

"Say, there's something else I wanted to tell you, Two Pockets."

"Ok, what's that?"

There was a knock at the door.

"Come in."

The door opened.

"Oh I'm sorry. I didn't realize you had company. I can come back later."

"Don't leave on my account, Miss Sissy. I suspect you're here for the same reason I am."

"So, you know?"

"Let's just say a little birdy told me something."

"Who would that be?"

"I can't reveal my sources."

"What're you two talking about?"

"Sorry, Two Pockets. Go ahead Sissy. It's big news. It's your news."

"Ok. You don't have to move if you don't want to, Tommy."

"What? Why's that?"

Tommy Two Pockets
And the Posse of the Marsh

"Because the Mouillee Rest Home has a new director."

"What? Who?"

"Me."

"You? Really? Well, that's great news, but what about the Griz?"

"She was escorted off the premises this morning during Julio's service by Hank and board members. That's why I was called away."

"What happened?"

"To tell you the truth, I'm at a loss here. Mr. McCorkle and Mrs. Shumate took me into the board room and offered me the position effective immediately. They wanted an answer on the spot. I said yes. I accept. They told me it was confidential about what happened to Ms. Haverhill, so I'm in the dark. They also told me that any construction on the porches was stopped. But, you knew that, didn't you, Captain Dougherty?"

"Hmmmm......"

"You did, didn't you?"

Cap stood there staring out the window at the marsh with a hint of a smile on his face.

"What did you have to do with this Captain?"

"I plead the 5th."

Tommy Two Pockets
And the Posse of the Marsh

"So you did have something to do with this."

"Again, I plead the 5th."

Sissy stood back and then gave Captain Dougherty a big hug.

"I don't know what you did, but thank you."

"The 5th still applies, but you're quite welcome. And you will be an outstanding administrator for the Home. There will be a lot of excitement once the word gets out. Actually, I'm surprised it hasn't already."

"Well, they purposely did it during Jeopardy, so everyone was preoccupied."

"Ha. Wonderful."

"Well, how about it, Tommy? Wanna stay around?"

"No. I don't think so, Sissy. This place never was for me, and I know you'll make it better, but that cabin on Fricke Island looks pretty good to me."

"I understand, but if the time comes you need us, please come back."

"I will, Sissy. I promise."

By the time supper rolled around, the prevailing rumor was that Ms. Haverhill was removed from her position because she was providing suicide pills to the residents and trying to kill them all off to sell the property and make a golf course.

Tommy Two Pockets
And the Posse of the Marsh

Of course, Tommy did what he could to feed the rumors. It was a special treat for his last day at the Mouillee Rest Home.

Chapter 41 - Island Days

"We've got some great seats right out here on the Veranda, and it's a beautiful evening. The Twin's Special tonight is Turtle Bisque. I had some today, and it is really good! Kim will be your waitress. She'll be right over."

Tommy walked back to the cash register.

"How was everything tonight?"

"Great as usual."

"Happy to hear that. That'll be $16.58."

Tommy's days were full on Fricke Island. He was usually up at dawn and had his coffee on the cabin porch overlooking the inlet. Julio's cane sat by the oversized bench he would sit on. Sometimes he would be joined by Matt, who came to pick him up for a day at the Marina. They would often lose track of time talking about the old days and what Sonny was like as a child.

Tommy would banter with the boaters while he pumped their fuel or helped carry supplies from the Marina store. He would make his way back to the cabin by mid-afternoon for a nap before heading to Beanie's Sand Bar and Grill for his supper and to help as the host. His reputation was growing, and the regulars called him Two Pockets. He loved it.

Tommy looked forward to the weekends. Alex came over on Friday evenings and bunked with Tommy until Sunday afternoon. Saturday, they helped Mickey with his customers on the head boat. They had anywhere up to 25 people on the boat fishing mainly for perch. Tommy and Alex would spend the day baiting hooks, untangling lines, cleaning fish, and tossing insults at Mickey and the customers. They got good tips.

Sundays were the best, as they reserved that time just for them. Sometimes they took a Jon boat out into the marsh and fished. Other times Alex would take Tommy into Detroit to watch the Tigers play. But their special times were when they just walked out on the point past Beanie's Sand Bar and Grill with a six-pack and watched the boats and all the wildlife. They sat on the bench that the Twins moved from the Mouillee Rest Home. Julio's bench. Soon everyone was calling the spot Julio's Point.

"What are you thinking, Tommy?"

Alex couldn't bring himself to call him Dad after all the years of calling someone else that. Tommy got it and didn't mind.

"I don't think I've been this happy since before World War II with you, your mother, and Trudy."

"Yeah, but doesn't it make you sad? All those years?"

"It used to. And it did when you first showed up, but nah. Not now. How 'bout you?"

"I guess I've been more curious than sad. I've had a good life and was lucky to be adopted by the Springsteads. But I do miss my wife. Do you miss mom?"

"Yeah, I never found anyone to take her place. Not that I was lookin'. I would have felt guilty like I was cheating on her."

Tommy Two Pockets
And the Posse of the Marsh

With that, they both popped the tops to another Stroh's and sat in silence, happy to be with each other.

Mabel became a regular visitor to the island. When Sissy came out to see her family, she made a point of bringing her along. She and Fiona became friends, and sometimes Mabel would stay at the Big House with Fiona and her second husband, Jake, for a few nights. On those nights when Tommy didn't have to fill in at Beanie's, they took a bottle of wine and headed out to Julio's Point, stared at the stars, and reminisced.

"Suds and Mooch keep asking me when they will get to come out and go fishing. I keep telling them you'll get back to me, and you never do."

"Yeah, you're right. Let me talk to Mickey and see when we can do it."

"When are you going to do that?"

"Don't worry, I will."

"When?"

"I said I will."

"When?"

"Geez, you'd think you were my wife."

"Heaven forbid......When?"

"Oh, for crying out loud. I'll talk to him first thing in the morning. I'm going out with him on a small charter."

Tommy Two Pockets
And the Posse of the Marsh

"Yeah, I know. I'm on it too."

"You can be a real pain sometimes, Mabel!"

"I learned from the best, Two Pockets."

Mickey had an opening the following Wednesday.

Chapter 42 - Fishing Posse

Alex got away from his contract position at the Navy Air Station north of Detroit for the day. Mickey wanted him to run one of the big Jon boats for the *Posse of the Marsh* fishing trip. Mickey knew where smallmouth bass were congregated in fairly shallow water near weed beds with a gravel bottom, and Jon boats were perfect for this type of fishing.

Each boat was geared to handle up to four people with cushioned high back seats. Mickey took Mabel, Cap, and Mooch, while Alex took Tommy and Suds. After leaving Fricke Island they headed south toward Black's Bay. Once they passed the mouth of the bay, they continued another four miles to the weedy gravel beds. They then set up and began to drift fish, bouncing a jig off the bottom.

The weather cooperated with a slight breeze that would push the drifting boats from north to south along the half-mile strctch.

The fishing started out slow, but as soon as they drifted over some shallow ridges, the fishing was fast and furious. The smallies were averaging around 5 lbs., with some reaching 7 or 8 lbs.

Suds was starting to get frustrated as he could not tell the difference between the jig bouncing off the bottom or a hit.

"I need worms. Never catch anything without worms."

"Use your worm, Suds."

Tommy Two Pockets
And the Posse of the Marsh

"Stuff it, Two Pockets. Come on, haven't we got any live bait? A minnow or something?"

"Be patient, Suds. And quit pulling your line in every time you think you feel something. Your odds of catching a fish go up dramatically if you have your lure in the water....... Aw gee, Suds. Not again!"

Suds yanked back on his line and got all tangled up in it as the lure came flying into him.

"Haven't you ever fished before, Suds?"

"Yeah. With live bait."

Tommy got him untangled and said,

"Look Suds, just let the jig bounce off the bottom and when a fish hits, it'll pull so hard you'll know it. Now cast it out a little ways and let it bounce off the bottom."

"Aw, this is a waste of time....Ho...ho....holy.....Shiiiiiii....."

The rod bent over double and line was running out of the reel.

"It's a monster.... It's a monster.... What is it Two Pockets?"

"My guess is it's a fish. Keep the rod tip up. Don't let it get under the boat."

"I know, I know!!"

"If you know, why is the rod tip in the water?"

Tommy Two Pockets
And the Posse of the Marsh

"I can't.... Whoooaaaah!!!"

"Put your hand in front of the reel and put the butt of the rod on your hip and keep the tip up."

"Ok,ok,ok,ok,ok."

Alex used the electric trolling motor to keep Suds in a good position to fight the fish. Mickey saw what was happening and had everyone reel in while he steered his boat over to help.

"What do you think he's got on Tommy?"

"If it's a smallie, it's a monster."

"I told you, hmmmfff, I told you it's a, hmmmffff, monster."

"What do you think it is, Mickey?"

"Well if it's what I think it is, we're going to be here a while."

"I know what it is. I caught one out here about 65 or so years ago."

"You did not Mabel. That was Old Man Black's grandson."

"Did too, Two Pockets! He lost it, I got it."

"Yeah, ok you got it."

"Got what Miss Mabel?"

"Sturgeon."

Tommy Two Pockets
And the Posse of the Marsh

"That's what I'm thinking this is. Tommy, if this goes on any longer you'll have to cut the line."

"What? No way, Mickey! You ain't cutting this line......Hmmmffff....Two Pockets. I'm either gonna eat him or put him on my wall. Maybe.........Hmmmffff.......Maybe both."

"You can't, Mr. Sutherland. They're protected in these waters. We have to let it go."

"Yeah but.........Hmmmmmmfffff......You don't know what it is until you see it."

"I know what it is. Cut it Tommy."

Suds started crying out.

"No....no.....no......"

As Tommy reached for the line it went slack.

"Reel it in Suds, Fast. He's heading to the boat."

By now Mickey had maneuvered close to them and watched the 70 lb. plus sturgeon come up next to his boat. He was able to guide it into a fish cradle and position it in the water so everyone could see the trophy Suds had caught.

"Wow great job, Mr. Sutherland."

"Why can't I take him home."

"I can't do that. You'd get in trouble and I'd lose my job."

Tommy Two Pockets
And the Posse of the Marsh

"Damn! That's what you get for bringing a game warden with you fishing!"

"Let me take some pictures and we'll let her go. Mr. Mooch, take the camera and let me hold the fish out. Mr Sutherland, lean into it so we get you in the picture. A little more....wait not....oooooh!"

After they managed to get Suds back in the boat they revived the Sturgeon and released it.

"Did you get any pictures Mr. Mooch?"

"Oh yeah. Going in and coming out. Plenty."

"What about the fish?"

"Ah....well......we'll see."

"I need to pee."

"That's what the bucket is for Miss Mabel."

"The what?"

"The bucket. We'll turn our backs."

"I ain't pissing in no bucket on no boat with a bunch of men. I've got my reputation to think about."

"That train left the station years ago, Mabel."

"Up yours, Two Pockets."

Tommy Two Pockets
And the Posse of the Marsh

"Well Miss Mabel, you don't have to use the bucket. You can hang over the side."

"What? Are you crazy? No...No get me to shore. I'll go on shore. Now! Get me to shore and you better hurry."

"Ah....ok there's a small point off the end of the sandbar up ahead. We can land there."

"Hurry!"

"Ok. Ok."

Both boats continued to head south to the sandbar Mickey knew about. Suds was drying out pretty quick, but found he too needed to relieve himself. Once they landed, they all piled out of the boats and headed into the sumac growth for some privacy. Mabel went deep into the small island away from everyone else. After 15 minutes Tommy yelled,

"Hey Mabel. You need some help?"

She didn't answer.

"I'm gonna go see what's up with her."

"I'll come with you, Tommy."

"Yeah, ok Mickey. The rest of you stay put."

Of course they all decided to go with him. After they'd gone about 50 yards into the sumac they found Mabel leaning against a tree and breathing hard.

"Mabel, what's wrong with you?"

Tommy Two Pockets
And the Posse of the Marsh

She looked at Tommy and pointed behind her.

"What? What is it?"

"We're back."

"What?"

"The island. Crow Island."

"Are you sure? This doesn't look at all how I remember it."

"These little islands and the marsh have changed a lot since you were kids, Tommy."

"I'm sure Mickey, but still. What did you see, Mabel?"

"The cabin.... The shed."

"Really?"

Tommy started walking in that direction. The sumac had taken over the island, but appeared to have been burned back recently.

"Was there a fire here, Mickey?"

"Last year. Happens in the marsh from time to time. Nature's way of cleansing and renewal."

They found the charred walls of the cabin that were still intact, as was the shed although two of the walls had fallen in. The outhouse was gone.

Tommy Two Pockets
And the Posse of the Marsh

"I wanna go in and look around."

"I don't know Tommy, it doesn't look safe."

"I'll be alright Mickey."

As he pushed on the door it fell off the hinges and into the small cabin. Part of the roof had caved in, and a family of raccoons scurried up to the rafters and out. The memories came flooding back to Tommy.

"Keep an eye out, Mabel."

"For what?"

"Otis."

"Otis is dead, Two Pockets."

"Ah.....yeah...well you never know."

"Come on Tommy, cut it out."

"Just keep an eye out for him, damn it!!!"

"Don't worry Tommy, I'll stand guard."

"Thanks, Cap."

Everyone stayed by the door as Tommy and Mickey looked around.

"What's this?"

Tommy Two Pockets
And the Posse of the Marsh

Between the deteriorated bed frame and the wall there appeared to be some old clothes lying on the floor. Tommy pushed the frame aside and nudged the clothes with his foot.

"Geez!"

"What?"

"Bones. There's bones."

As Tommy bent down the clothes fell apart to his touch, exposing the skeleton beneath them. Mickey knelt down beside him.

"That's a man. Look at the size of the bones and the hands. What's that?"

Tommy moved the shirt apart and there in the chest held up by some rib bones was what appeared to be a knife.

"I think he was stabbed and by the looks of it, in the heart."

"The handle of the knife is broken. I think I recognize it. It looks like the same one I took from Otis 65 years ago. Do you think someone did this to him, Mickey?"

"That would be my guess."

"I think its Otis."

"Why do you think that?"

"The clothes. The size of him. Just being here like this. I'm gonna check his pockets."

Tommy Two Pockets
And the Posse of the Marsh

Tommy found an old army wallet in his trousers.

"Well he wasn't a rich man. Got $3 on him. Here's a driver's license from 1939. Says his name is ah......Earl Campbell."

"Anything else?"

"Some receipts. One from a shell station for $2.34 and one from Rosie's diner for 68 cents. Hmm....There was a Rosie's diner kiddy corner from our apartment in Wyandotte."

Then Tommy found a small card with an address written on it. 334 Maple Ave. Apt 2c. He dropped everything and slumped to the floor.

"Tommy what is it? Tommy?"

"That was our address. Oh God no, no, no, no, no, no. Otis Pies you Son of a Bitch! Where's Alex? Alex!!!"

Alex made his way into the cabin.

"I'm here Tommy what? What is it?"

"I think I know what happened to Meg. I know what happened to your mother. Oh God!"

"What?"

"Otis. He said he was gonna make me hurt in ways I could never imagine."

"Oh....oh..... I remember what that man told me the night mom disappeared. He said if I ever see my daddy to tell him to remember. I said remember what? He said just tell him to

298

remember. I told him my daddy's with the angels. Then he laughed and said nah, I don't think so. Just tell him to remember."

Tommy staggered out of the cabin, leaned against a charred sycamore tree and started wailing. He was soon kneeling on the ground as Mabel put her arms around him. Alex joined them and through his tears said,

"So Dad, you think he took Mom? Is that what you think happened? He took her and brought her here?"

Tommy tried to pull himself together enough to answer him.

"Yep. That son of a bitch is still hurting me 65 years later. He killed Mr. Perkins, 5x5, Julio, and......Meg. And.....and....who knows who else."

Tommy stood up and held his fists to the sky and yelled.

What did I do, God?! What did I do?! Why did you put Otis in my life?! If he's not in hell, put him there! You owe me that, God! You owe me that!"

Chapter 43 - Investigation

Tommy started searching the cabin looking for any sign of Meg as Mickey contacted the Sheriff's department on the radio.

"Tommy, you really shouldn't be in here, this is a crime scene."

"Leave me alone Mickey."

"Come on Tommy, let's get you back and let the authorities handle this."

"I'm not going anywhere, now leave me alone."

"Please Tommy, it's going to start raining within the hour and I don't have enough rain gear for everyone. And really, you shouldn't be messing around here."

Tommy turned to Mickey, grabbed his shirt, and yelled in his face.

"I mean it! Leave me alone!"

Mickey took his wrists and forced him to let go.

"Alright, I have a couple of rain ponchos in my boat. I'll give you one and then I'm taking everyone else back."

"Get one for me too, Mickey."

"Okay Alex. You stay here with him and I'll pile everyone into my boat and get them back. In the meantime watch him so he doesn't get hurt. I'm going to meet the Deputies back at the Fricke Island Marina and guide them out here."

"Any chance you can bring some food back with you? I think it's going to be a long day."

"Sure Alex, I'll call back to the marina and have them make up some sandwiches and whatever. Just watch him."

"Yeah."

By noon Mickey was back with two Monroe County Sheriff deputies.

"Mr. Tupoc, you and your son are going to have to leave the island. We'll take it from here."

"I'm staying."

"You're just going to be in the way."

"I'm staying."

"Don't make me…"

"Leave him alone, Russ. It'll be ok."

"But, Harv, we can't let him muck around here."

"Russ, this probably happened over 40 years ago. We ain't gonna catch the killer who's probably already dead. I'm sure there's nothing he can do to hinder what little we'll be able to find anyway. Just let him be."

"Alright Harv, but it's your butt, not mine."

Tommy Two Pockets
And the Posse of the Marsh

"Whatever, Russ."

"It's Tommy Two Pockets, right?"

"Yeah, that's what they call me."

"I bet you knew my grandfather. Dennis Zmolek. Constable Zmolek."

"5x5? You're 5x5's grandson?"

"Yeah, I heard they called him that. He was killed by Otis Pies."

"I know. I was there."

"What was he like?"

"Otis or your grandpa?"

"Let's start with my grandpa."

"I liked him. Everybody liked him. Tough, but fair. No bullshit. He could hold his own. I remember his funeral like it was yesterday. Sad day. Lota tears."

"Now tell me about Otis."

"Mean as they come. Strong as an ox. He had a son Lumpy that he used to beat the hell out of until our posse rescued him. That's what started this whole thing with Otis. If that's Otis in there, and I think it is regardless of what that driver's license says, whoever stuck him got lucky."

Tommy Two Pockets
And the Posse of the Marsh

"Ok, so you think this is Otis and he brought your wife here, when did you think?"

"I'm guessing in 1942. That's when she disappeared. I found our old address on a card in his wallet."

"So you think he killed her out here?"

"Yes."

"Well, it doesn't appear that anyone has been out here since he was stabbed and it seems that would have happened in the 40's, based on that driver's license. It said his name was Earl Campbell, but it was pretty easy back then to get a fake license. I took a quick look around the island and I didn't find any remnants of a boat, so I know I'm speculating here, but I'm guessing that whoever did Otis in, left the island."

"Are you saying that he didn't kill Meg? Could Meg have done that?"

"Not saying that at all. I'm just saying that the killer isn't on the island."

"But what if he did kill Meg and buried her here?"

"He could have taken her life anywhere, not just here. If he did, not much chance of finding out, but I'll have the dogs brought out in the next few days and have them sniff around. See if anything shows up. You good with that?"

"Yeah, thanks. That would be good. I've just gotta know."

"Ok, so in the meantime, let's have Alex take you back to Fricke Island, and I'll let you know what we find. Ok?"

Tommy Two Pockets
And the Posse of the Marsh

"Yeah, ok. But you'll let me know what you'll find."

"Of course."

Chapter 44 - Julio's Point

Mabel found Tommy on Julio's bench.

"Are you just gonna sit out here and waste away what little time you've got left on this earth feeling sorry for yourself? Alex called me and told me he's worried about you. Fiona says you've been begging off work and she's worried you're not eating enough. You can't fix what happened, Tommy. It's over."

Tommy looked over at her and then stared past her to a flock of pelicans that were making a big circle before landing off of Julio's Point.

"That's the first time I've ever seen them around here."

"What?"

"The pelicans."

"The what? Pelicans? What pelicans?"

"The ones that just landed behind you."

"Where?"

"Off to your left."

"Those are pelicans?"

"Well, they ain't robins!"

"Good. Smart ass. That's the Tommy we know and love. You gotta pull yourself out of this funk you're in, Tommy. You're scaring us all. Are you listening to me?"

"I heard you Mabel. Pull myself out of what?"

"Well, this funk you're in."

"What funk is that, Mabel?"

"What I said. You're not eating and you're begging off of work and Alex is worried about you."

"Well stop worrying. I'm alright. I've just been thinking, that's all. Sometimes a body just needs to think through some things before they can get on with other things. That's all. I ain't gonna do myself in or anything if that's what you're thinking."

"That is what I'm thinking. Or you're just gonna let yourself go."

"Oh stop it..........I've just been thinking about my life and how, even though I lost Meg and Trudy and Alex for all those years, my life hasn't been all that bad. I never got rich or did anything to change the world, but I think I mattered. In some small way, I mattered. And maybe that's all life is supposed to be about."

"You matter to me, and I know you mattered to Lumpy. You know? He wouldn't let anyone ever say a bad word about you or anybody that was in the Posse, for that matter. He never forgot what you did for him. Are you sure you're alright?"

Tommy Two Pockets
And the Posse of the Marsh

"Positive. Like I said, I just needed time to think. And I thought a lot about Otis. He's probably in hell somewhere thinking he won. But he didn't. If he thinks he ruined me, he didn't. Did he hurt me? Yeah, of course he did. But I'm not the one who's gonna spend eternity in hell."

"You sure about that, Tommy?"

"I know I ain't been a regular church goer or anything, but I still remember Father Mac telling me about that little verse in the Bible, John 3:16. That says it all. And I believe that, Mabel. Always have. Always will. I hope you do too, Mabel. I know we're from rough stock, but I believe God takes care of us. That's what I believe. That's my hope."

Mabel took Tommy's hand as they sat and watched the pelicans bob up and down as they floated by. After a while Tommy said, "You like beaver burgers, Mabel?"

"Beaver burgers? What?"

"Beaver burgers. The twins have some ready for the grill. Let's go have one."

"I ain't eatin' no beaver, Tommy Two Pockets."

"Don't knock it till you try it."

"Gross."

"Well, maybe you'd like some of the muskrat they got. I'm pretty sure it's fresh."

"Oh, you think I won't eat muskrat? We did when we were kids. Didn't kill me then. Don't think it will now."

Tommy Two Pockets
And the Posse of the Marsh

"I'll stick with the beaver."

"Yeah, you do that."

Chapter 45 - Cap Comes Through

"There you are, Tommy Two Pockets. I've been looking all over this island for you. Oh, is that one of the Twins' beaver burgers you're eatin'?"

"You betcha. I talked Mabel into trying one and well, look at her."

"Da gooo...."

Mabel had a mouth full and was ready to take another bite when Fiona said,

"Did they tell you how they make them? They get them to be nice and tender by mixing them with the liver, heart, and the beaver's tongue. How they figured that out, I'll..............whoops!"

Mabel spit the burger out all across the picnic table.

"I guess I shouldn't have told you that part," Fiona said as she stifled a laugh.

As Mabel excused herself to go to the bathroom, Tommy asked,

"Why were you looking for me, Fiona?"

"Oh yeah. Captain Dougherty is here. Says he's got something important to talk to you about. He's up at the big house flirting with the help. You finish up while I fetch Mabel, and we'll take the golf cart back."

Tommy Two Pockets
And the Posse of the Marsh

The Big House was built during the heyday of prohibition using funds the Fricke family acquired working with the Lacavoli Family smuggling Canadian whiskey across the border. The 7,500 sq ft house is not only Fiona and her husband Jake's home, but part of it was converted to Fricke Island Enterprises, consisting of the Marina, Beanie's Sand Bar Grill, FIE distribution, and various other small business interests. When they pulled up to the house, Captain Dougherty was sitting on the porch overlooking the marina and the vast marsh.

"Hey Cap! I hear you're looking for me. What are you doing out here?"

"Yes well, they gently suggested I wait for you out here. I think I may have been too big of a distraction for the bookkeeping staff. A certain Miss Dorothy, to be exact."

He raised his eyebrows up and down and gave a wink.

"So, what brings you all the way out here?"

"Well Tommy, I told you I would see if I could get into the records at the Evangelical Home. I've got some results, and I also took the liberty to hire a private detective to do a little further digging."

"A private detective? Sorry Cap, but I don't have the funds to pay for a PI."

"Ah....but I do, and you're not to worry yourself about that. That's an order!"

"Aye aye, Cap. Like I always say, you're the best. So, what did you find out?"

Tommy Two Pockets
And the Posse of the Marsh

"It's all right here in this folder. Now I told my niece that we will not share this with anyone else. Is that clear?"

"Aye aye, Cap."

"Alright. Now let me give you a summary of the highlights. Some very interesting highlights, I might add."

"Ok tell me."

"Well, your daughter Trudy only spent one week at the Evangelical Home. She was put into foster care, and the foster family ended up adopting her one year later. Her last name at that point was Venier, and she grew up - are you ready for this? - in Gibraltar just north of here."

"What?"

"That's right, Gibraltar."

"You mean I lived within 20 miles of her and never knew it?"

"Well Tommy, you still do."

"What? You know where she lives?"

"I have an address."

"I've got to call Alex."

"I've taken the liberty of already doing that, Tommy. I knew you'd want to see her as soon as I told you. Alex should be here any time."

Tommy Two Pockets
And the Posse of the Marsh

"I can't believe this. First Alex and now Trudy. Do you know anything more about her than the address?"

"Yes, but I think I'll let you find out more when you see her."

"Cap. How can I ever thank you?"

"There is one more thing that you need to know. There's a handwritten note in the file. Brace yourself, Tommy."

"Ok, What?"

"About four years after Alex and Trudy were brought to the home, a lady showed up looking for them. Said she was their mother, but she had no proof or identification as to who she was, so they dismissed her as some sort of crack pot."

Tommy slumped down in his seat, put his hands to his face, and started to cry. Captain Dougherty put his hand on Tommy's shoulder and said,

"There's more, Tommy. The note also talked about several scars on the lady's face and she walked with two canes, dragging her left foot as she shuffled along."

"Oh..........oh..........oh."

"Yeah......I suspect it was Meg that put that knife in Otis."

"But if it was Meg, why didn't she find me?"

"I don't know, Tommy, but didn't she think you were dead? Isn't that what Alex said?"

Tommy Two Pockets
And the Posse of the Marsh

"Yeah, yeah I suppose."

"Look, Tommy, Alex is going to be here any second. Try to pull yourself together before he gets here."

"Does he know?"

"Just about Trudy."

"Thanks again Cap."

Chapter 46 - The Find

Alex and Tommy drove the short distance to Gibraltar looking for 326 Horseshoe Drive. They found an older brownstone ranch in a small subdivision next to a canal that flowed into the Detroit River.

"Are you ready for this, Tommy?"

"Yeah. How 'bout you?"

"Sure. Let's go."

Alex knocked on the door, which quickly opened.

"What the hell are you doing here?"

"Well......I came looking.........."

"Looking for what, Two Pockets?"

"Griz? Why are you here?"

"I live here, dumb ass."

"But..."

"But what?"

"But....but"

"But, but what? Spit it out."

"Does someone named Trudy live here? We're looking for Trudy."

Tommy Two Pockets
And the Posse of the Marsh

She gave him a long look, shook her head, and grunted.

"Of course."

"Can I talk to her?"

"What's this about?"

"Can I talk to her?"

"You really are a dumb shit aren't you, Two Pockets? You are talking to her."

"What? No. Really? You're....Trudy? But your name is Grizelda."

"My name is not Grizelda and never has been Grizelda, and nobody ever called me that until you showed up at the home."

"What?"

"Yeah, I heard you were the one that started calling me that, and pretty soon everyone was calling me that behind my back. That is except for you and your fruitcake friends. Now you wanna tell me what this is all about? My soap is about to start."

"Can we sit down, Griz, I mean......Trudy?"

"Just tell me what you want and then leave."

"Let me take this, Tommy. Hi Trudy. I'm Alex."

"So?"

Tommy Two Pockets
And the Posse of the Marsh

"So.......I'm your brother."

She looked at him like he was crazy.

"Yeah, right. I don't have a brother."

"Yes you do, and it appears Tommy is our father."

"Two Pockets my father? What? Ok, you're both off your nut."

"Do you know you were adopted?"

"Adopted? I'm not adopted. Where'd you come up with that? Did this old fool put you up to this? Bad enough you cost me my job. Now you come around here playing games with me."

"It's not a game. You were adopted during the war when you were two years old by the Venier's."

"Adopted by the Venier's? Where did you come up with that? They were my real parents. You're wasting my time."

She started to close the door, but Alex put his arm out to stop her and with his other hand held out the file.

"It's all right here. This is a file from the Evangelical Home in Detroit. Read it, please. If you don't believe it after you've read it, we'll leave you alone."

She looked back and forth between the two of them, grabbed the folder, and walked into the house. They followed her in and sat with her at the dining room table as she started reading.

316

Tommy Two Pockets
And the Posse of the Marsh

"Yeah, this doesn't prove anything. This could be anyone. I'm not sure you two have the...................."

She stopped talking and read the handwritten note.

"My God. This note. I know the lady they're talking about."

"You knew her?"

Trudy had a puzzled look on her face as she stared at the note.

"I know her."

"You know her? She's alive?"

"She became friends with my mom when I was, oh I don't know. Maybe six or seven. She used to babysit me and take me to the movies and shopping and........She'd buy me pretty things and go on vacations with us and go to my band concerts and the plays I was in. She became my best friend......... She still is. She wasn't my real aunt, but I call her Auntie Meg."

Tommy rubbed his forehead as tears formed in the corner of his eyes.

"Trudy......She's your mother. My wife."

A look of shock came across her face as her eyes darted back and forth between them.

"My mother? This is too much."

"She's alive? Do you know where she is?"

Tommy Two Pockets
And the Posse of the Marsh

"I don't understand any of this. How? Why? What?"

"Trudy, please. Do you know where she is?"

"Yes."

"Where Trudy? Where?"

"Wait, wait, wait, wait a minute. This is a hoax right, Two Pockets? Did my ex put you up to this? That bastard. Get out! Get out right now!"

"No. No wait....Do you have a scar on your leg?"

"What?"

"Do you have a scar on your leg? Your right leg? On your thigh?"

"What? Did that bastard Chester tell you that?"

"I don't know who Chester is, but there is a scar, isn't there? I know how you got that scar. Do you know how you got that scar?"

"Ok smart guy, how did I get that scar?"

"A dog. We were having a picnic and a dog bit you and we took you to the doctor and got stitches, and then we went for ice cream after. So, do you remem......."

"Chocolate vanilla swirl."

"Yes Trudy. Chocolate vanilla swirl. That was everybody's favorite ice cream at the General Store."

318

Tommy Two Pockets
And the Posse of the Marsh

"I remember the dog and the ice cream, but that's all."

Trudy leaned back in her chair and stared out a window.

"I guess this explains why I didn't find any baby pictures of me when I went through mom's things after she died. I thought that was kind of strange."

"Trudy. Where is Meg?"

"Hm....Meg."

"Yes. Where is she? Can you tell me?"

"Yeah. Let me get some shoes on and I'll take you there. I've gotta hear this from her."

Chapter 47 - Family

As they were riding the elevator up to the 5th floor of the Albright Nursing Center Trudy said,

"By the way, I work here. I'm the night shift supervisor. Only job I could get after I got fired."

"Sorry, Gri....Trudy. But I didn't have anything to do with that."

"Sure."

"I didn't, really."

They walked down the corridor and stood outside of room 517.

"Let me go in first. You two wait out here. Let me break it to her."

As she opened the door they heard,

"Oh Trudy, I'm so happy to see you. But why are you here so early? It's only a little past noon, isn't it? Is everything alright?"

As Trudy tried to close the door, Tommy stepped into the room.

"You were supposed to wait in the hall."

"Well, hello. And who are you?"

Tommy Two Pockets
And the Posse of the Marsh

Tommy slowly went down to one knee as he stared at the old lady in the wheelchair. He recognized the beautiful hazel eyes that still sparkled in the scarred, withered face that looked at him. He took the hand that she reluctantly gave him and kissed it.

"Trudy? What......?"

"You're still a beauty Meg. A beauty. I'm so.....so....sorry."

With that, Tommy started sobbing. Deep, heavy sobs as he buried his head in her lap.

"Trudy? Trudy? What is going on? Who is this?"

By now Trudy was sitting on the bed bawling.

"Will someone tell me what is going on? And who are you?"

Alex came into the room, knelt down beside her, and held her other hand.

"Meg. I'm Alex.........your son."

Her mouth fell open and she started to breathe rapidly. Trudy grabbed an oxygen mask off the stand behind her and put it on her face.

"Trudy! Trudy!"

"Auntie Meg. Calm down. Look at me. Calm down. It's ok. It's ok."

She started to get her breath back.

Tommy Two Pockets
And the Posse of the Marsh

"That's better. That's better. Auntie Meg. I have a question to ask you."

"What?"

"Do you know how I got the scar on my leg?"

She stared at her with a puzzled look.

"Do you know how I got the scar on my leg?"

"Ahhh........Yes."

"How?"

"Well....Well....mmmm.....A dog bit you."

"Were you there when it happened?"

"Oh lord. How did you.......mmmm....."

"Sweetheart, please. Were you there?"

Tears were flowing down Meg's cheeks as she looked at Trudy, searching for the right answer and a way to tell her. She finally looked down and whispered.

"Yes. I was there......... I was there, Trudy"

Tommy looked up at her.

"So was I."

Tommy Two Pockets
And the Posse of the Marsh

Meg stared at his face as she took the oxygen mask away. She then put her hands on either side of his face and looked deep into his eyes.

"This can't be. How? Tommy?"

Tommy put his hands on hers and shook his head up and down.

"Yes, my dear. I'm Tommy."

"But.....But....you're dead."

"No."

"Yes you are. The Navy. The telegram. They said you were dead."

"No. It was a mistake."

"A mistake? Mistake? Where have you been? I don't understand."

"I'm trying to understand too, Meg. I'm trying."

Trudy put her hand on Meg's shoulder.

"So Auntie Meg, you're my Mother and this man is really my Father?"

"Yes Trudy. I'm sorry. I don't know what to say. It's just that......"

"Why didn't you tell me? After all these years? You know you could tell me anything."

Tommy Two Pockets
And the Posse of the Marsh

"I've tried so many times, but I.......I don't know. When I first found you with the Venier's and saw how well you were doing and how they could give you so much more than I ever could, I...I...I was a broken woman, Trudy. Do you understand that? Broken. I had nothing and never would have anything. You know I barely scraped by all these years. I was lucky to get that bookkeeping job at Maxwell's where they could keep me in the back room so I wouldn't scare their customers."

"Oh, Auntie Meg. I wish you wouldn't say that. I always thought you were beautiful. You weren't going to scare anyone by a few scars."

"It wasn't just the scars on my face, Trudy. It was the scars in my soul. I just didn't want to deal with too many people. You know that."

"But you always treated me and Mom and Dad so kind. You know we loved you. Did they know?"

"Betsy was pretty intuitive. She figured it out, and we both decided not to tell you until after they were both dead or I was dead. Either way."

"But Auntie Meg. They've both been dead for over 10 years."

"I know. I don't know what to say. But now you know."

Meg started questioning Alex about his life and what happened to him. She had tried to find him, but never could. Trudy was also full of questions, as was Alex. While the three of them kept up a non-stop q and a, Tommy sat in a chair off in the corner and took it all in. He watched as Meg would exhibit the little quirks in her speech or the way she would

324

Tommy Two Pockets
And the Posse of the Marsh

brush back a curl just as she had done 45 years earlier. A little giggle or the raise of her eyebrows in excitement at the bits and pieces of information she gleaned from the two of them. And when she looked over at Tommy and smiled, his heart melted just like it had all those years ago in the shipyard. To him, she was still perfect. Finally, as evening descended, Trudy said,

"I'm going to take Alex down to the cafeteria for a bit to eat. We'll bring something back for you, Tommy. Auntie Meg's dinner should be here shortly. Will you two be ok alone?"

"Oh I think so, sweetie."

When they left, Tommy picked up his chair and put it next to Meg's wheelchair.

"I suppose you've remarried, Tommy."

"No. Never did. I just couldn't bring myself to find anyone else. Did you?"

"No. Never had a boyfriend or anything."

"So we're still married then."

"I think so, yes. But I went by the last name of Evans."

"Why Evans?"

"Well because I thought Meg Evans just rolled off your lips."

"Why didn't you use Tupoc? I probably could have found you then."

Tommy Two Pockets
And the Posse of the Marsh

"I didn't know you were alive and looking for me, besides....."

She turned her head and started to cry again.

"Besides, if I used Tupoc he could have found me. That's why I didn't want to tell Trudy her last name at birth. So he couldn't find us."

"Who couldn't find you? Otis? Was it Otis Pies?"

"I never knew his name. I really don't want to talk about it. I just can't."

"Ok. I understand. Can I just ask a few questions?"

"I don't know."

"Did he take you to an island in the marsh?"

After a long pause while she looked out the window, she said,

"Yes, but that's all I want to say about it."

"Ok, but let me just tell you this. We found a body in a cabin in the marsh. He had a knife with a broken handle sticking out of his chest."

She looked at him with a surprised look on her face.

"What?"

"So you don't know about that?"

She closed her eyes, put her hands up to her chin, and finally said,

Tommy Two Pockets
And the Posse of the Marsh

"He had been using that knife to cut my face and he would say "Two Pockets won't love you now." Every day he would put a new cut on my face. He broke my hip and my knee cap. I could hardly get around. Then one evening, I saw the knife lying under some rags. I don't know why, but I picked it up and threw it in his direction. He shouted at me as I went out the door and drug my left side down to the canoe and got in. I thought maybe I hurt him, because he never came after me. I didn't know. All I wanted to do was get away from him. It took me two days to get out of the marsh. Well, that's what I think it was, I'm not really sure. All I know is I woke up at the Seaway Hospital. Some duck hunters found me."

"What did the police say?"

"Well...........they really didn't say anything, because I didn't say anything. I was afraid that he was still going to come after me and oh, Tommy................ I spent four years in an asylum. I just couldn't..."

Tommy leaned into her and put his arms around her as she sobbed into his shoulder.

"Oh Tommy, it was like I looked into the eyes of the devil himself. He took me to hell, Tommy. I've seen hell and I don't ever want to go there..........But he knew you, Tommy. He never said why. But he knew you. Did you do something to him?"

Tommy started to tell her the story of he and the *Posse of the Marsh* and Lumpy and Black's Bay when Trudy and Alex came back.

Tommy Two Pockets
And the Posse of the Marsh

"Alex, I need some time with your mother. Can you two leave us for a little bit?"

"Of course. Let's go up to my office, big brother. I've got a lot of questions for you."

Tommy spent the next hour explaining in detail what took place in 1920 at Black's Bay.

"And after so long, we thought he was dead. Everybody did. If I'd known he was still alive, I would have never left you alone. It's all my fault. I don't know how I can make this better. I don't know what to do. I know there is no way you can forgive me, Meg. I understand."

Meg took Tommy's hands and rubbed them as she looked in his eyes for an answer.

"I'm not sure what to say or think right now, Tommy. I mean, I thought you were dead. I had given up trying to find Alex. I was just satisfied that I was able to be around Trudy and still am. But I know this, Tommy Tupoc, the fear and........I guess anguish that I've had for the last 45 years feels like it's somehow leaving me. I feel like this is a miracle. I'm feeling something I haven't felt since 1942. Joy. Real Joy. Tell me this is real, Tommy. Tell me I'm not dreaming."

Tommy put his hand on her face and kissed her on the lips. A deep, loving kiss as their tears mixed together.

Chapter 48 - Time for Sleep

He lay there thinking about the past five years as his mind drifted in and out of sleep. He declared that 1988 was the best year of his life. Meg. Sweet Meg. He got her for another year. A full, glorious year. He watched her come back to life and noticed how she would do her best to make herself pretty for him, even though it wasn't necessary. The hours they would spend on Julio's Point just holding hands and enjoying their quiet talks. He missed her and smiled when he thought of her. She would visit him in his dreams.

Sometimes she was the young, vibrant girl he first knew, and other times she would dazzle him with her beauty as she would rise from the wheelchair and put her arms around him. He knew it wouldn't be long before he would join her again. He was ready. He knew it was time.

He started thinking about the gazebo the Twins had quickly put up on Julio's Point with the wheelchair ramp for Meg. The many evenings that they, along with Alex and Trudy, would spend grilling their catch from their day out on Lake Erie. He could hear Meg laugh as she would reel in a nice Walleye and tease Tommy, because he was getting skunked. He loved it. He loved the memory.

He loved that he got to know Alex, who was quickly replacing Julio as his best friend and confidant. And he especially loved that underneath the rough and tough exterior of the Griz, he found Trudy. And though there were a lot of wounds that needed healing, he thought she slowly and grudgingly loved him just like he loved her.

His mind drifted to the 4th of July that year when Trudy, Alex, and his children Alex jr. and Steph spent the long

Tommy Two Pockets
And the Posse of the Marsh

weekend on the island. Fiona made accommodations for everyone including Mabel and Meg at the Big House. They all gathered at the gazebo and watched the grand fireworks display the Twins put together. They talked and laughed and cried and hugged and sang and joked until sunrise when Fiona showed up with a tray of caramel rolls and coffee. How they were all able to stay up all night like that was a mystery to him. Was it a premonition of heaven, where you can't pull yourself away from the ones you love?

He thought about how that magical year ended as Meg caught a cold that turned into pneumonia that turned into her funeral. He could feel tears on his face as he recalled her last words before her last breath. "Don't be long, Tommy." Her funeral was one of several over the past five years.

First it was Suds due to Alzheimer's. Then it was Mooch who had a massive heart attack. At least it was quick. Finally, Mabel. The cancer didn't linger, and took his little buddy fast. He hoped she found Lumpy in heaven. Cap was the only one left, still carrying on like always. Still giving his lectures. Still being a great man.

He reflected on the four years after Meg died. He felt like he was in limbo. He still got together with Alex and Trudy every week and he still helped around Fricke Island, but he knew time was getting short.

And here he was in bed, feeling helpless. He didn't really mind. He was just ready for it to be over.

Two weeks earlier, he had slipped on the ice as he was coming out of his cabin and lay there for two hours in the sub-freezing cold before Mickey came looking for him. He had broken his hip, hand, and collar bone in the fall. Once he

Tommy Two Pockets
And the Posse of the Marsh

was in the hospital he had a major stroke that went undetected during the night. Now he lay in the hospital bed, unable to use his left side while his right side was broken from the fall.

He was surprised that he was actually pretty comfortable and figured they must have him on some pretty good meds. He just knew that he didn't want to be here like this very long.

"Mr. Tupoc......Tommy.....Can you hear me? Can you hear me Tommy?"

He opened his eyes and looked at her.

"There you are. Do you know who I am?"

He nodded his head and tried to say Miss Sissy, but the words would not come.

"Tommy, I am so sorry to see you like this."

She moved close to his head and whispered in his ear

"There is a better way.
A peaceful way.
You don't have to continue suffering."

Made in United States
Orlando, FL
19 November 2022

24752841R00198